The Proposal

"If you read anything this Cl͏ stories make it perfect for any age and any stage of family. You will feel the Christmas magic."

Torinda D,
Stay at home mom,
Edmonton Alberta)

A Hair Cut for Santa

"The imagery can make you feel like you are living right there in the moment! You can feel the warmth, magic and even the crisp wind while taking that ride on the Snowmobiles!"

Marcus V,
Network Consultant,
Edmonton Alberta

Oh My, Santa Does the Splits

"I love the touch of culture and relatability. That you can clearly envision what is going on because you have been to the "Edmonton's Festival of Trees" and how even past the stories it provokes memories with my own children. The additions of demographics is a very nice touch bringing this story to wonder if it truly happened"

Virginia D,
E.A.,
Alberta

Wake Up, Karrie! Santa was Here

"I really enjoyed the story of Wake Up Karrie! Santa was Here. It brought back lots of memories of our dog that laid under the Christmas tree pretending to guard the presents. Our dog would always make sure the presents were safe until Christmas morning. Very enjoyable read an exciting story.

J Cooper,
Richmond Hill, Ontario

Also by the Author

Santa's Christmas Memoirs Volume 1

Santa's Christmas Memoirs

Volume 2

Robin L. White

WHITE, Robin L
Santa's Christmas Memoirs Volume 2

Published by Robin White, Edmonton, Canada

   W: www.santaswhitechristmas.ca
   T: @SantaWhiteChr1
   F: Santa's White Christmas

ISBN 978-1-77354-177-8

Publication assistance and digital printing in Canada by

PUBLISHING
PageMaster.ca

Thank you

Santa and Mrs. Claus are standing in front of the window in their living room watching the sun slowly set in the west on Christmas night. The fire was crackling in the fire box and the smell of birch wood burning filled the living room. The Christmas lights were glowing on the Christmas tree. Both Santa and Mrs. Claus are so very tired from delivering presents to all the families of the world. It was nice to be home and surrounded by every one that lives at the North Pole.

Santa bent down to pick up Christmas Cookie. He then gave her to Mrs. Claus to pet. Santa then put his arm around Mrs. Claus as they moved closer together. The sound of many voices could be heard coming from Christmas town.

The elves of Christmas town were singing a Christmas song. Each elf carried a candle as they walked from Christmas town to the castle on North Pole lane. They are all singing "We wish you a Merry Christmas."

We would like to thank all the readers of this book.

From all of us at the North pole

Santa and Mrs. Claus

And

Christmas Cookie

Merry Christmas and Happy New Year.

Acknowledgments:

Jen Durette. of Jen's Photographer.
Family Lifestyle Photographer.
Lamont County, Alberta, Canada
Phone 1-(780)-235-8565
Mrs. Claus and I would like to thank you for the great looking
pictures. you have provided for this book cover. As well your
Professionalism is outstanding.

Contents

CHAPTER 1

He is the Real Santa Claus

As I was sitting in my chair, seeing all of the bright and shining faces, there was this little girl that was standing next to her parents. She kept looking at me, as I was looking back at her. Well, it was her turn to come and see me; Mrs. Claus talked to her for a moment, then brought her up. As she stood in front of me, she was still looking at my beard to see if I had straps under my hat that was holding my beard up. The little girl then looked at Mrs. Claus and asked, "Is that real?" Both Mrs. Claus and I started to smile, and Mrs. Claus said, "Why don't we both give it a very little tug?" Mrs. Claus told the little girl, "On the count of three, we will both give it a little tug."

I said, "Hey, wait a minute, don't I have anything to say about this?" They both said, "No!" in sync.

Mrs. Claus started the count down and on two, I closed my eyes and when they got to three, Mrs. Claus gave a little tug and the little girl gave a great BIG tug. The next thing I knew, she was running towards her parents yelling, "He is the real Santa, Mom and Dad! He is the real Santa." As the three of them were leaving, the little girl was still telling her parents that my beard was real and I'm the real Santa With a tear in my eye, I waved at the little girl, and Mrs. Claus was off to bring another little one to see me.

He Is The Real Santa Claus

```
K  W  E  S  S  S  X  N  D  H  I  G  D  Q  U
A  L  V  Y  T  Y  F  E  B  V  M  J  U  M  M
R  G  B  Y  E  N  U  V  F  Z  A  L  A  O  E
Y  E  P  E  G  C  E  A  N  Q  G  O  E  U  Y
X  G  A  P  A  H  B  R  J  C  I  T  S  V  B
Z  C  C  L  M  R  J  M  A  T  N  D  L  U  E
Q  E  M  J  G  O  D  R  U  P  L  O  X  R  W
J  Z  I  C  S  N  W  S  G  I  V  I  Q  I  E
Z  D  U  E  I  I  U  C  V  U  Q  H  V  B  V
L  S  A  O  E  Z  R  L  B  O  T  S  F  R  A
R  O  I  G  X  A  W  A  S  T  R  A  P  S  W
I  V  O  L  N  T  T  U  E  K  M  N  N  N  T
G  Q  A  K  O  I  U  S  V  T  E  T  X  I  X
J  X  T  K  I  O  L  N  E  Q  P  A  A  J  B
W  X  G  P  E  N  C  L  V  J  M  H  X  S  M
J  J  R  C  B  F  G  K  E  S  R  X  E  J  L
Y  O  A  H  R  H  T  S  B  Y  U  U  G  K  M
```

LOOKING	BEARD	STRAPS
REAL	SYNCHRONIZATION	NO
TUG	TEAR	EYE
WAVE	YELLING	MRS CLAUS
SANTA	GIRL	PARENTS

Robin White

CHAPTER 2

A New Sleigh for Mrs. Claus

With the Christmas season over, the elves were taking it easy. Aunty Joe was back home, and Mrs. Claus was busy with her computer, checking all of the events that Santa and she had attended. Santa decided to go down to the sled shop to look at making a new sled for Mrs. Claus. Santa knew she wanted her own sled so she could go down to the village to do some shopping from time to time. When he walked into the sled office, Jim was sitting at his desk and eating a reindeer cupcake. Jim was just about to take a sip of hot chocolate, when he noticed Santa was standing at his door. Jim stood up and welcomed Santa to his office. Jim asked, "So, Santa, what can I do for you?" Santa was busy looking at the box of reindeer cupcakes they are a real hit. Mrs. Claus only made them after Christmas to say, "Thank you for all of your hard work with the Christmas that just passed." Santa looked back towards Jim, then replied, "I would like to build a new sled for Mrs. Claus so she could go into the village from time to time for shopping. I would like it to be strong, but lightweight and it has to be two-reindeer power and white in colour!" Jim put his right hand behind his head and started to scratch, then turned towards the cupboard that had some blueprints in it. As Jim was looking for the design that Santa wanted, Santa was still looking at the reindeer cupcakes. He decided to help Jim look for the blueprints for Mrs. Claus' new sled. After a few minutes of looking, Jim found them.

As both of them looked at the blueprints, Santa said, "We will need to make a couple of changes here," pointing to a couple of spots on the blueprints, "to make it the right size for Mrs. Claus." Jim agreed with Santa. Santa then shook Jim's hand and asked when would the new sled be ready? Jim replied, "In three or four days, Santa." Santa then started to smile and said, "Bye, Jim." and left the shop. As Santa was walking back to the castle, he stopped to watch some elves having a snowball fight. As Santa was about to leave to meet up with Mrs. Claus, the elves decided to have some fun. Santa felt something hit the back of his coat and belt all at the same time. Santa thought, "Oh, okay, bring it's on now!" Mrs. Claus was coming out of the castle and she witnessed the snowballs hitting Santa. She hit the snow running she was not going to miss a good snowball fight! She got in behind the elves that were throwing snowballs at Santa. Santa started to laugh, and he bent down and grabbed some snow and made a perfect snowball. After a few minutes, the snowball fight ended, and yes, the Clauses won! As the Clauses were helping the elves up and making sure they were fine, they decided they would go for a walk and see how everyone was and how their Christmas had gone.

Jingles came running up to Santa and Mrs. Claus. He had a message for Santa. Jingles then stopped right in front of Santa and asked him to bend down, as he had a message from Jim. So Santa bent down on one knee to hear the message. Mrs. Claus also bent down to hear the message, but it was very short. Santa stood back up, looked at his wife and said, "Well, my dear, I have to go and see Jim for a few minutes, it should not take long." Santa whispered a special message in her ear. She looked at him and replied, "I will see you later, Santa."

Santa could hear the elves working hard on Mrs. Claus' sled. They already had the panels cut out and were about to put it together. Santa was impressed by how fast Jim and his elves worked. Santa was about to ask Jim where the runners for the sled were, when Jim pointed to the shop across the street. Santa looked through the window; he could see some short, blue flashes of light. Santa knew that the elves in the welding shop were finishing up the runners. Santa looked at Jim and asked, "What do you need?" Jim replied to Santa, "The sled will be ready tonight and we can have it in the reindeer barn after 5 p.m." Santa replied, "That's great news!" Santa had a smile on his face. He had wanted to give Mrs. Claus a new sled for a while. Santa said goodbye to Jim, "I will see you in the reindeer barn at 5 p.m. with Mrs. Claus." Santa headed back to the castle. He felt like a young man that had just bought a horse and buggy for his wife at the local blacksmith shop.

Jingles tugged on Santa's coat, then said, "We have to head for the toy shop now, Santa, to say thank you and have some hot chocolate and that new dessert that Mrs. Claus made for everyone, snowman cupcakes, then we can head to the new appointment you just made for Mrs. Claus' new ride." Santa nodded, as he and Jingles headed for the toy factory. All of the elves were heading the same direction as Santa. As Santa was about to climb the stairs to the toy shop, he heard his name being called by his loving wife, Mrs. Claus, so Santa waited for her. He put out his arm and helped her up the stairs; at the top of the stairs, Santa held the door open for her. The clock in the town square chimed it was now 3 p.m. Santa looked back at it and started to smile. As the Clauses walked into the large toy factory, there was a thundering ovation of clapping and cheering coming from the elves. At that moment, the overhead doors opened just high enough for Mrs. Claus' bakers and hot chocolate makers to come into the toy factory, so Mrs. Claus could pass out the cupcakes and Santa could pour the hot chocolate, saying thank you for the help everyone gave throughout the year. As the event was coming to an end, Jingles came and tugged on Santa's coat again to let him know that everything was ready. This little piece of news put a smile on Santa's face.

As the last cupcake and cup of hot chocolate was being handed out, the clock in the town square rang five times. Santa went over to Mrs. Claus to let her know that they had another event to attend. Mrs. Claus looked at Santa as if to say, "What other event do we have to attend?" Santa put out his right arm and Mrs. Claus put in her left arm, and off they went to their next event. Mrs. Claus asked, "Santa, what is our next event?" Santa replied, "We have to go to the reindeer barn for a few minutes, because there is a new reindeer about to be born." Mrs. Claus liked to see a new birth now and then. As they approached the front of the barn, a reporter from Aunty Joe's Christmas newspaper was there to take pictures of the new arrival and get a story as well for the next edition. As the Clauses entered the barn, Mrs. Claus looked up to see a bright white sled sitting in the white room. She was speechless and looked over at Santa and Jim, who was standing next to Santa.

Santa then said, "Here is your very own sleigh, my dear. I hope you enjoy flying her. She is a two-reindeer power sled." Mrs. Claus was speechless. Tears started to come down her cheeks, and she was happy. Two of Santa's elves brought Dancer and Prancer out and hooked them up to the brand-new sled. After the two were hooked to the sled, Santa helped Mrs. Claus in and handed her the reins.

Santa was about to hook up his seat belt when Mrs. Claus yelled, "On Dancer, on Prancer!" and she snapped the reins. In a moment's notice, the two reindeers were off and gaining speed. Santa's head snapped back, and his body got pushed into the seat of the sled. Mrs. Claus snapped the reins once again to make the reindeer go faster. Santa was hanging on to his hat with one hand and the front of the sled with the other hand. Mrs. Claus was trying to level off, but the sled was going up and down. Mrs. Claus was having fun learning how to fly her new sled. Santa yelled, "Pull up, you're heading for the castle!" Mrs. Claus pulled back on the reins and up the sled went, but she pulled back just a little too far and to the left; she and the reindeer and Santa were doing a barrel roll.

There was a loud scratching noise coming from the bottom of the sled as the runners was scraping on the side of the castle. Mrs. Claus pulled the reins to the right as she was coming out of the roll. Santa said, "We need to go back, Mrs. Claus. We need to get you some non-flying reindeer for now." So, Mrs. Claus headed back to the barn with her new sled, but she wanted to make a full circle around Christmas Town. After she made the fly-by, she headed for the barn and made a nice soft landing, and the reindeer walked into the barn. Santa did not look well as the elves help him out of the sled. Mrs. Claus was ready to go for another ride, but it was getting dark. She would have to wait until tomorrow. She walked over and helped the elves bring Santa back to the castle. Mrs. Claus said, "Thank you, Santa, for my very own sled," and gave him a big hug and a kiss on the cheek.

Robin White

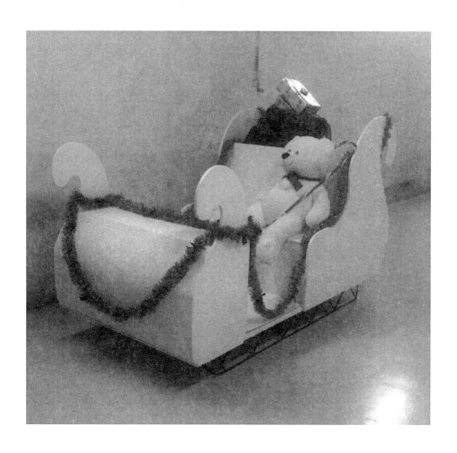

A New Sleigh for Mrs. Claus

```
N  Z  K  S  Y  C  C  I  G  X  X  D  M  A  F
X  S  K  Y  I  G  O  C  F  S  H  G  E  S  I
C  N  O  V  R  W  M  T  S  A  Y  F  M  W  G
P  O  B  E  T  A  L  O  C  O  H  C  T  O  H
P  W  P  X  T  U  J  Z  U  S  Q  H  L  R  T
F  M  D  M  F  R  E  T  U  P  M  O  C  N  L
T  A  H  A  T  N  A  S  L  G  M  V  C  Q  H
Q  N  Q  L  G  V  L  U  E  Z  Z  N  R  X  E
S  T  F  K  S  L  E  I  G  H  E  A  A  P  X
S  E  S  T  N  I  R  P  E  U  L  B  S  P  N
E  A  Y  A  O  Q  L  V  B  W  R  G  H  M  R
N  H  R  I  W  N  S  E  K  A  C  P  U  C  A
T  I  Z  J  B  Z  C  K  L  E  Z  L  D  S  E
I  S  Q  P  A  T  W  I  G  Y  Q  K  G  G  L
W  Q  U  E  L  T  S  A  C  M  I  Z  C  V  G
I  H  T  G  L  B  A  R  R  E  L  R  O  L  L
Y  A  Q  F  N  E  W  X  M  H  Y  E  I  K  Y
```

COMPUTER	BLUEPRINTS	SNOWBALL
FIGHT	NEW	SLEIGH
WITNESS	CUPCAKES	SNOWMAN
HOTCHOCOLATE	SANTA HAT	BARREL ROLL
CASTLE	CRASH	LEARN

Robin White

Give Our Baby Elf a Name

Aunty Joe was at home, drinking her favourite hot drink, hot cocoa, when she decided to call her cookie counting buddy Blinky. This put a smile on her face, because of the time Mrs. Claus caught them counting her chocolate chip cookies; there were some damaged ones, so Aunty Joe and Blinky ate them. That was when Mrs. Claus came in! Well, this seemed like so long ago, when Blinky was a young elf. Aunty Joe also wanted to see if Blinky had had her baby yet.

The phone kept ringing at Winky and Blinky's home. Aunty Joe thought maybe Blinky was at the kennel, or the doctor's office, or she could be with Mrs. Claus; there were so many places that elf could be. The phone was still ringing, and there was still no answer when Aunty Joe hung up the phone. She went into her bedroom to her walk-in closet, opened the door and walked into the back, where there was a shiny metal box with an old-fashioned lock on the side of it. The box was on the upper shelf. She looked up at it, placed her right hand on her mouth and paused; she then reached up and took the box down. She went into her bedroom and placed the shiny metal box with the old-fashioned lock on her bed.

Aunty Joe went and got the magic key that was in a secret place in her house and, with a gold skeleton key in her hand, headed back to her bedroom to open the lock on the box. When she put the key into the lock, a white light came from inside the keyhole, opening the lock. The only thing special about this key is that Aunty Joe was one of three people that could open this magic box, and Santa and Mrs. Claus were the other two. Aunty Joe opened the box to a red telephone inside it. On the telephone base was a red Christmas bulb. Aunty Joe picked up the receiver of the telephone. A few seconds later, the red Christmas bulb lit up and on the other end was the North Pole operator. The operator answered, "Hello, Aunty Joe, North Pole operator here, how can I direct your call?"

Aunty Joe then said, "Hello, Jingle Bells, I'm looking for Blinky and I was wondering if she has had the baby elf yet?"

There was a pause, then Jingle Bells answered Aunty Joe's question. "Well, A.J., as of right now, we are all on baby elf watch. The hospital is on standby and Winky is a nervous wreck, but you know how those elf men are. I heard Blinky say she had to teach Winky how to boil water and have the suitcase by the front door. The snowmobile is all gassed up, and the sidecar is hooked up to the snowmobile. It has a sleeping bag in it with a lot of blankets and pillows. Oh yes, did you hear that Blinky's mom has moved into their home and is now staying there? It's driving Winky crazy. You know that old saying, 'Too many elves in the kitchen burn the Christmas fruitcake." Both Jingle Bells and Aunty Joe started to laugh. Then Jingle Bells said, "You're not going to guess what Winky did. Blinky almost lost her elf ears, it must have been really bad." Jingle Bells then said, "A.J., can you please hold on to your Christmas ornaments? I have a few calls to take care of, so please hold." It did not take long for Jingle Bells to clear the switchboard and get back to Aunty Joe's line. Jingle Bells then said, "Well, A.J., I'm back." Aunty Joe said, "Hello. So what happened to make Blinky so mad at Winky?" Jingle Bells replied, "Well! It all started a couple of days ago when Blinky's mother was cleaning up the house.

She was in the living room, cleaning off the coffee table, and she found a sheet of paper folded in half. It was a plan and the title on the top read 'Give our baby elf a name contest'! It was to have everyone at the North Pole play 'Name the Baby Elf'. The winner could name the baby elf; here are the rules. Every elf had to guess the date, the exact time of birth and exact weight of the baby elf. This is the best part. It would have cost a hard-working elf two dollars, and you can guess how many elves we have up here now!" Aunty Joe bit her lower lip trying not to laugh. Jingle Bells said, "Well, A.J., guess who heard about this pool? She was not happy! And in turn, it made him even less happy, and the last one lost her mind!" Jingle Bells paused to take a breath when Aunty Joe was about to answer. Jingle Bells said, "You guessed it: Mrs. Claus, Santa and

Blinky." Jingle Bells then said, "Well, Winky is in front of Santa, Mrs. Claus and Blinky right now in the Great Hall!" Aunty Joe said, "Oh my!" Jingle Bells said, "The last time that room was used was over 150 years ago and they had to bring in lots of elves to clean that hall. I feel sorry for Winky. I can see the Clauses may go easy on him, but then he may be removed from helping Santa deliver presents on Christmas Eve. We think that the Clauses just might let Blinky deal with this. I would not want to be in that elf's shoes in the next hour on the way home. I can see Blinky giving Winky the silent treatment until they get home. And when Blinky gets him home..."

Aunty Joe could not hold back anymore; she started to laugh, and her laugh was a deep belly laugh as if her belly was full of jelly, just like Santa. Then Jingle Bells said, "So, Aunty Joe, I can't connect you right now. I have a note from Santa: 'Hold all our calls until we are done dealing with this matter!' Aunty Joe said, "I will call back later. Thank you for bringing me up to speed on what's going on with Blinky. Goodbye!" Jingle Bells disconnected A.J. from her switchboard. Aunty Joe hung up the red phone, closed the lid and relocked it, then placed it back in her walk-in closet. Aunty Joe was thinking as she was coming out of the closet, "That igloo garage is going to feel like the Bahamas before Blinky will let him back into the house!"

Give Our Baby Elf A Name

```
Q  O  S  T  N  E  M  A  N  R  O  F  C  X  B
Y  O  Y  K  J  W  C  W  Y  T  C  Y  T  A  D
F  L  F  E  M  C  A  T  H  G  S  L  H  A  O
O  G  J  A  O  U  O  Y  B  G  A  A  O  P  P
V  I  F  Y  R  J  I  N  S  L  M  G  E  T  K
J  P  P  U  T  G  Y  R  T  A  Q  R  E  D  L
K  K  F  J  S  O  A  T  S  E  A  D  X  F  A
L  E  M  S  D  E  S  A  N  T  S  N  E  A  S
M  Y  J  J  C  K  A  R  O  U  D  T  Z  T  P
B  V  E  L  M  Y  C  R  L  X  A  Z  O  O  Q
E  N  O  H  P  E  L  E  T  X  V  C  V  K  R
Q  K  L  B  P  R  M  S  O  Y  B  A  B  K  P
K  L  C  A  J  M  E  A  W  E  R  T  D  G  L
G  M  N  E  J  A  A  S  N  N  L  O  O  O  P
W  Y  Q  C  R  J  A  G  E  G  V  V  M  F  H
U  R  R  T  D  W  G  W  I  N  N  E  R  B  P
P  C  K  R  M  C  Y  Z  B  C  T  C  O  Z  T
```

AUNTYJOE	TELEPHONE	OPERATOR
NAME	BABY	EARS
IGLOO	ORNAMENTS	WRECK
KEY	MAGIC	CONTEST
WINNER	PRESENT	BAHAMAS

CHAPTER 4

A Trip to the Hospital

Hello, one and all, Dexter here, I'm Blinky's big brother. I have a story for you, so gather everyone around.It started one cold and snowy night. Blinky and Winky were sound asleep in their beds when Blinky let out a blood-curdling scream that sent Winky falling out of bed. He hit his head on the nightstand. Winky yelled out, "What? What's the matter?" Blinky turned on the light that was next to her bed. Winky looked forward with his eye mask still on his face. Blinky yelled out, "My water broke, and the baby is coming!" Winky was crawling back into bed when Blinky's words finally hit home. Off came the eye mask. Winky looked right at Blinky and said, "Did you say the baby is coming?" Blinky said, "Yes!" with a growl in her voice as waves of pain started to come through her body. Winky said, "The baby's room is not ready yet!" Blinky just looked at Winky and gave him 'the look'! Winky said, "Don't panic, Blinky, okay? Don't panic! I have everything under control!" Winky jumped, but not all of him made it out of his bed; his right foot caught the footboard, sending him flying onto the floor near the closet doors. Winky jumped up and said, "Don't worry, Blinky, I have everything under control!" as he waved his hands in the air in front of him. Blinky heard a cry and "Ouch" coming from the living room. It was Winky stubbing his baby toe on the corner of the couch. Winky yelled out, "Don't worry, Blinky, I have everything under control!" as he limped to the coat room.

Winky grabbed two snowsuits and helped Blinky into hers, then he put her snow boots on her feet. Winky said, "Don't panic, Blinky, okay? Don't panic! I have everything under control!" Then he got into his winter gear and helped Blinky to the snowmobile sidecar that was parked in the garage next to the house. Winky started the snowmobile up with the turn of a key. He was about to put the snowmobile into gear when Blinky yelled out, "STOP! THE GARAGE DOORS ARE STILL CLOSED!" Blinky was waving both her hands in front of her. Winky said, "Oh yes, I know they are, honey." Winky climbed off of the snowmobile and opened the garage doors, then headed back into the house and came out with two suitcases for Blinky. Winky put both suitcases on Blinky so she could carry them. Winky jumped back onto the seat of the snowmobile and off they went to the hospital, which was on the other side of Christmas Town. About halfway to the hospital, the snowmobile started to act up, losing power and finally stopped in front of Santa's Kennel. Winky was yelling at the snowmobile, "Come on, come on, start, come on!" He turned the key until the battery died! A few more waves of pain went through Blinky. Winky opened the gas cap and the gas tank was empty. Blinky yelled at Winky, "Go and get a sled. GET CANYON'S TEAM, NOW!"

I was in the dog kennel, watching all of the Santa's malamutes, when there was someone banging on the front door. I left the office and headed for the front door to see who it was, banging and yelling at this hour of the morning. I opened the door to see my brother-in-law standing in front of me, and my sister sitting in a sidecar hooked to a snowmobile. I then asked, "Hey, guys, what's going on and what are you doing here?" Winky asked, "Dexter, where is your snowmobile?" I replied, "It's at home. I walked to work tonight, being such a nice night and all, you know." Winky asked, "Do you have any gasoline for the snowmobiles?" I said, "Nope! Santa does not allow that stuff here, you know that, Winky." Blinky yelled at Winky and me, "Go and get a sled, and GET CANYON'S TEAM NOW, and I mean NOW!"

Both Winky and I ran into the building to get everything in order. It did not take us long to get the team ready. Winky helped Blinky out of the sidecar and into the sled, put the suitcases at the front and was about to grab the handles and step on the runners, when Blinky had another wave of pain. She yelled, "Chocolate chip cookies!" Well, that is Canyon and his teammate's favourite words, and they took off. Poor Winky, he went flying backwards into a snowdrift! Winky got up in a hurry and started to chase the sled as fast as his legs would take him. Canyon and his teammates were starting to gain speed, as Winky had just about caught the back of the sled. He had both hands on the handles and was about to jump onto the runners when, you guessed it, Blinky had another wave of pain and she yelled, "Chocolate chip cookies!" and the team of malamutes started to run faster. Winky was being dragged behind the sled and hanging on for elf life!

As the team of malamutes raced across Christmas Town, poor Winky's snow boots were making a trail behind the sled. They were heading for Santa and Mrs. Claus' castle. Then the team turned back towards the centre of Christmas Town. Canyon and his teammates started to slow down. This was when Winky needed to pull himself up and get his feet onto the runners. He was just about to put his left foot onto the runners when the team stopped all of a sudden. This sent Winky into the back of the sled and winded him. It took Winky a few seconds to catch his breath, and he then climbed onto the back of the sled and tied himself to the back of the sled, then called out, "Chocolate chip cookies!" The team of malamutes started to run again; this time they were heading for North Pole Hospital. As the team approached the hospital, the sled hit a bump; this sent a wave of pain through Blinky and she cried out "Chocolate chip cookies!" You guessed it again, Canyon and his teammates started to run faster! This sent both Winky and Blinky's heads back for a second.

Winky looked forward and there was the hospital right in front of them, so he applied the brake. As he was pushing down on the wooden pedal, the wood snapped off of the sled and Winky looked back as the wooden brake tumbled in the snow behind them. Winky had only one option left to stop the sled, and that was throw the parking brake, which was a hook that was on a rope. When the sled was stopped, the driver would take this hook and put it into the hardened snow, and that would prevent the team from leaving. Winky yelled towards Blinky, "What do we have to say to stop Canyon and the team from running?" Blinky looked towards Winky and wondered, "Why would he ask a question like that?" Then Blinky knew why Winky asked that question. Blinky looked back at Winky and said, "Please tell me that you two did not grab the sled that had an 'out of order' sign on the front? Did that brake pedal snap off?" That sled was to go out for repair on its brakes! Blinky looked for the number on the side of the sled and it said, "Santa 7." The front of the hospital was getting closer and closer. Blinky looked back at Winky, reached down and grabbed the emergency brake and was about to throw it, but it was too late for him to throw it.

The glass sliding doors to the front of the hospital opened up, and Canyon and his teammates drove the sled right through the front door and stopped at the front desk, where Nurse Anne Marie Tinsel was sitting at the desk, doing some paperwork. Canyon jumped up with his front paws and looked eye-to-eye; his mouth was wide open, and he was breathing heavily on the nurse. Another wave of pain hit Blinky and she cried out, "Christmas trees!" All of the malamutes sat down in the front lobby of the hospital. Nurse Tinsel got out of her chair and ran towards the sled to see what the matter with Blinky was. Winky then cried out, "Nurse, I'm having a baby!" Both Blinky and Nurse Tinsel just looked at Winky, then Winky said, "No, Nurse, WE are having a baby, my wife and I!" This put a smile on both Blinky and Nurse Tinsel's faces.

Nurse Tinsel got up, ran back to her desk, pushed a red emergency button and headed back towards the sled. Before she got back to the sled, help was coming through the side door that lead to the emergency room. Two nursing orderlies picked up Blinky and put her onto a stretcher and took her back to Emergency. Winky was about to follow when Nurse Tinsel tapped Winky on the left shoulder and stopped him from following Blinky into the emergency room. Winky's head turned towards the nurse, and she pointed at Canyon, his teammates and the sled that was parked in the front lobby they had to go! Winky then asked the nurse, "Can I use your phone?" Nurse Tinsel said, "Yes, after you park them outside in the sled parking zone!" She pointed with her arm straight out and her finger towards the front doors. Winky moved Canyon and his team out to the sled parking zone and came back into a waiting clipboard with a lot of papers on it.

Winky asked to use the phone again. He put the clipboard down on the desk. Nurse Tinsel pointed towards it and went back to her work. Winky picked up the receiver and started to dial the kennel. The line was busy. Winky put the receiver back in the cradle and Nurse Tinsel handed Winky the clipboard with a lot of papers to fill out for Blinky to be admitted Winky grabbed the telephone receiver one more time and dialed the kennel and got through to me. I answered the phone and said, "Hello, Santa's Kennel here, how can I help you?" Winky then said, "Hello, Dexter. Winky here. I need you to go and get your snowmobile and bring it to the hospital, and get Santa's dog team and bring them back to the kennel." I said, "Okay, Winky, I'm on my way. I called in Lenny to help us just in case. Lenny just arrived, so I'm on my way." Winky said, "Thank you," and hung up the telephone receiver.

Winky started on the paperwork that Nurse Tinsel gave him to do. As he was filling out the paperwork, he reached for his wallet to get Blinky's elf health care number and he remembered his wallet was on the desk in his office at home. Winky then ran back towards the nurse's desk to call me at the kennel before I left, but it was too late, I was already gone! Winky had to fill out the rest of the forms and handed the clipboard back to the nurse. I walked into the waiting room to find Winky holding three boxes of candy canes on his lap, rocking back and forth, getting ready to pass them out when his new child was born, as all fathers did at the North Pole. I just stood there for a moment and watched Winky rocking back and forth, as if he was waiting to see the principal in his outer office.

I asked, "Winky, any word yet?" Winky looked up at me and words just would not come out of his mouth. He was still rocking back and forth. I wanted to sit next to my brother-in-law, but I had to get Canyon and his teammates back to the kennel. I handed Winky the keys to my snowmobile and said, "Winky, the tank is full of gas and I will be back in a bit." Winky just nodded his head up and down, then looked down at his lap at the candy canes once again. The door to the maternity ward opened, and a nurse came out, carrying a bundle in a pink blanket. The nurse looked around the waiting room. Winky jumped up and ran over to see the new arrival and the head that was showing. Winky asked, "Nurse, is this my baby girl?" Then Winky looked down to see a baby reindeer in the blanket. Winky was about to faint, when the nurse said, "Your wife is still in labour, sir, this little one belongs to Dasher's family. Right, Daddy?" Dasher looked up and hurried over to the nurse, then looked down at his new daughter. Dasher then handed all the fathers in the waiting room a candy cane. Dasher followed the nurse out of the waiting room.

The clock on the wall was moving slowly in Winky's mind. Santa and Mrs. Claus came into the waiting room to see how Blinky was doing and to see how Winky was holding up. Mrs. Claus sat down next to Winky and asked, "Winky, how are you doing? And any word on how Blinky is doing?" Santa went over to the hot chocolate machine and was going to buy three cups of hot chocolate for them. As the machine dropped the last cup and started to make the hot chocolate, Nurse Tinsel came into the waiting room. In her arms was a blue blanket with a red Santa hat on the baby's head. Nurse Tinsel called Winky over and said, "Winky, come and meet your new son." The look on Winky's face was priceless. Santa started to laugh, "Ho, ho, ho," and Mrs. Claus had a smile on her face, her head cocked to the left just a bit and she said, "Congratulations, Winky, on the birth of your son."

Santa put down the hot chocolate and walked over to Winky, shook his hand and said, "Congratulations, Winky, it looks like it's time to break open a box of candy canes!" Winky put the three boxes down on the chair that he was sitting on, opened one and gave Santa, Mrs. Claus and Nurse Tinsel each one. Winky then asked, "Nurse Tinsel, how is my wife doing and is the baby okay?" Nurse Tinsel replied, "Everyone is doing just fine, and thank you for the candy cane."

A Trip to the Hospital

```
D  P  M  Y  V  I  L  C  N  F  T  F  Z  P  Q
E  I  O  W  K  V  G  H  T  D  A  Q  G  R  A
L  M  O  F  K  T  N  W  P  Y  H  I  K  I  M
S  Y  R  D  M  W  L  X  M  Q  M  R  D  N  E
R  A  G  L  C  T  K  P  E  I  K  O  O  C  Y
Y  R  N  D  A  E  D  I  X  Y  O  H  D  I  V
L  Q  I  I  N  A  R  H  L  L  O  G  B  P  X
N  D  T  H  D  M  E  C  H  R  Z  Y  A  A  A
A  J  I  Z  Y  L  H  E  R  E  R  H  B  L  I
N  Y  A  N  C  T  T  T  E  D  L  B  Y  S  J
N  V  W  N  A  I  A  A  I  R  O  P  T  O  U
E  R  K  C  N  D  F  L  N  O  R  T  O  F  X
M  W  O  T  E  O  Q  O  D  K  T  A  E  F  T
A  B  R  E  A  K  P  C  E  E  N  I  D  I  J
R  G  I  H  B  O  A  O  E  C  O  Q  S  C  F
I  F  Q  Z  K  T  I  H  R  Q  C  L  F  E  P
E  S  V  A  X  U  N  C  V  P  L  S  Y  E  V
```

SLED	CONTROL	CANDY CANE
ANNE-MARIE	WAITING ROOM	PRINCIPAL'S OFFICE
PAIN	CHOCOLATE CHIP	COOKIE
BABY TOE	REINDEER	TEAM
FATHER	ORDERLY	BREAK

CHAPTER 5

Oh My, Santa Does the Splits

Hi, my name is Jingles. I'm one of Santa's elves, and I have a true story about Santa for you to read, so grab a large, ice-cold glass of milk and some chocolate chip cookies, pull up a chair, get comfortable and enjoy this story.

One year, I was helping Santa at Edmonton's Festival of Trees. He was busy seeing all the little ones and hearing what they wanted for Christmas, when one of the local television stations came up to talk to Santa and myself. Well, after the interview was done, I spotted a little one that did not want to come near to see Santa. As Santa was talking to some little ones, I went to get the reporter and the camera crew and brought them back to Santa's Den. I said to them, "Come back, you have to see this!"

As Santa finished talking to the little ones and their parents, I had a smile on my face, to the point of almost bursting into laughter. I went over to see the mom and dad to talk to them. As I bent down to talk to the young man, he grabbed his mom's left leg and started to scream and cry, so I went and got our toy train and showed the young man that he could sit on this toy train in front of Santa. So the young man released his mother's leg and followed me to where I placed the train in front of Santa. Once the young man was sitting on the toy train and in place, I would let the parents know when to take the picture. I would count down from five, and when I hit the number one, they would take the picture.

Let the countdown begin! Five, four, three, two – Santa would then leave his big, comfy green chair and do the splits behind the little one that was looking at his parents as they took the picture!

One! There was a big flash from the camera. The reporter said, "Oh my, Santa does the splits!" Santa looked over to see the media recording what had just happened. He waved at them, and then bounced back into his chair. The little one turned his head back towards Santa to make sure he was still in his chair, and he had a smile on his face, thinking that he had beaten Santa out of another Christmas picture. The little one's father asked Santa if he had ever played hockey. Santa replied, "Why yes, I played goalie in the elf league reindeer division and we are in first place this year." Both of them started to laugh.

I looked over at Mom and she was smiling with a tear in her eye as she looked at the screen on the back of her camera, when the little one wanted to see the picture. She thanked us for getting his first Santa picture without him crying and fighting Santa. Mom showed Dad the picture, and as the three were leaving the Den, Mom bent down to show the little one his picture. He turned and gave Santa a dirty look and stuck out his tongue.

Santa then said in a very loud voice, "Ho, ho, ho! Merry Christmas!"

Oh My, Santa Does The Splits

```
J   I   N   G   L   E   S   U   E   X   S   C   H   I   C
N   N   H   D   L   D   G   G   I   J   T   N   Q   C   U
K   T   N   B   J   H   Q   N   L   S   I   R   C   G   S
E   E   F   D   H   U   Y   W   A   G   L   S   I   C   H
M   R   N   X   X   E   Q   O   O   S   P   Y   G   O   L
J   V   G   E   Y   B   A   D   G   W   S   C   A   L   P
L   I   U   P   T   O   Y   T   R   A   I   N   H   X   Z
R   E   C   O   R   D   I   N   G   C   G   Q   X   Q   Q
Z   W   A   R   V   H   U   U   W   I   Y   U   X   M   N
X   C   P   G   R   E   P   O   R   T   E   R   K   K   W
I   A   I   I   U   J   D   C   M   Q   E   S   Y   C   S
X   M   C   A   P   E   L   M   Z   N   Q   F   S   V   E
T   E   G   J   S   L   E   F   O   H   S   A   L   F   F
Q   R   G   U   M   D   M   I   J   N   N   S   O   D   L
Y   A   S   M   I   L   K   W   L   G   T   F   N   G   K
I   X   B   A   L   W   R   L   Z   J   T   O   W   I   M
P   L   D   K   E   E   Y   S   O   Y   R   B   N   J   P
```

JINGLES	EDMONTON	MILK
COUNTDOWN	CAMERA	FLASH
SPLITS	MEDIA	TOY TRAIN
RECORDING	LEAGUE	SMILE
INTERVIEW	REPORTER	GOALIE

Robin White

CHAPTER 6

The Proposal

With the snow falling gently outside and the sweet sound of "Silent Night" being played through the PA system, Mrs. Claus and myself were sitting in Santa's Den at the Edmonton Festival of Trees, seeing all of the fine children, when this young couple came up to see us. I noticed that the young man had pulled a small box out of his coat pocket, so I decided to help him. I got out of my chair and I winked at Mrs. Claus, which told her I was about to do some Santa magic. I told the young man to go down on one knee and stay there. I then moved over to the young lady and placed her standing in front of him; I took her left hand and placed into his left hand.

Mrs. Claus moved to stand behind the young lady. The young man opened the small box to reveal a diamond ring. The young man was going to ask the young lady to marry him! It took a few seconds, then the young man proposed. As I was standing behind him, looking at both of them, she started to cry and said, "Yes!" The young man looked up at me and I winked at him.

As they were putting their coats back on, I heard her say, "You planned this with the Clauses?"

As they left the den, I heard him say, "I wrote Santa a letter, asking him to bring you to me."

With a lit Christmas tree behind them, the young man placed his arms around her, he pulled her close to him and gave her a hug and a kiss, then they left our den.

The Proposal

```
J  E  Y  C  R  G  F  X  Z  A  D  N  A  W  S
O  E  P  N  X  J  G  Y  B  X  P  X  V  M  E
Q  N  P  V  D  D  P  C  D  E  N  N  A  L  P
L  K  A  H  E  R  C  R  I  N  G  L  S  Y  I
I  R  Q  I  Q  I  W  P  I  Q  L  T  K  S  I
K  Z  R  T  G  B  A  M  N  B  D  N  E  F  J
S  C  N  A  Z  Q  G  R  O  N  T  S  Q  W  E
N  R  M  P  J  N  J  X  A  E  U  B  B  Z  T
Z  Y  L  Q  P  E  C  H  M  A  G  F  U  F  S
C  K  E  D  X  M  T  S  L  A  P  I  U  R  W
Q  N  J  Y  N  F  G  C  A  T  N  T  A  W  I
H  I  Z  C  E  O  S  T  F  N  V  N  V  N  K
J  W  U  L  D  S  M  U  S  R  T  R  M  A  L
N  Q  I  Y  U  P  N  A  I  N  L  A  D  Y  R
C  P  X  L  Z  E  I  B  I  M  B  S  S  E  U
L  E  T  T  E  R  Q  E  W  D  P  Q  E  O  E
D  V  B  O  F  E  F  V  J  O  J  E  K  T  L
```

YES	CLAUSES	KNEE
SMALL BOX	MAGIC	LADY
MAN	LEFT HAND	DIAMOND
RING	SANTA'S	WINKY
CRIED	PLANNED	LETTER

Robin White

CHAPTER 7

Canyon Takes a Ride

Santa's elves were busy getting the big red sleigh ready for a flight. The elves were polishing it, as Santa likes his sleigh to shine from front to back, top to bottom, and every jingle bell tested and polished, and as for the reindeer, Doctor K9 was giving them all a thorough physical and afterwards they would be groomed. Up in Santa's office, his phone started to ring on his desk. Santa looked over and picked up the receiver. "Hello?" It was the kennel calling. The head dog master Blinky replied, "Hello, Santa. We need you to come down to the kennel right away, there is something you need to see." Santa replied, "Okay. I'm on my way down." Santa hung up the phone. He would go down to the kennels to see what the matter was. Within a few minutes, Santa walked into the kennels to see all the elves standing around Canyon's kennel as Doctor K-9 was checking over the big malamute. He could hear some hums and haws. Santa was waiting for the doctor to finish when Blinky noticed Santa and headed towards him. At that moment, Doctor K-9 came out of Canyon's kennel and was happy to see Santa there. The doctor wanted to give Santa the news about Canyon himself.

The doctor said, "Good news, Santa, I have checked him over from nose to tail, from the bottom of his paws to the tips of his ears, and he is perfectly fine. I think he misses someone and we both know who!" Santa looked into Canyon's kennel and said, "Yes, Doctor, I agree. In a few days, we are heading to the big city to go and get her." The doctor looked at Blinky and asked, "How much has he eaten and drank in last two days?" Blinky replied, "Nothing, Doctor!"

Santa and the doctor looked at each other, and then Santa said,

"Okay, we go tonight. I will have Mrs. Claus call her to have her meet us at our landing field." Santa walked over to the phone in the kennel and picked up the receiver and called Mrs. Claus to let her know what was going on, and to tell Aunty Joe what was going on with Canyon. Santa hung up the phone and went back to talk with the doctor and Blinky. Santa looked over at Blinky and said, "Blinky, I think you should come with us as well, just in case." She started to smile and said, "Yes, Santa."

Mrs. Claus was in her office. She called Aunty Joe to let her know that they were coming for her and why. "Hello?" This startled Mrs. Claus when she heard someone on the other end of the line, because her mind was thinking about Canyon and Aunty Joe. "Oh hi, A.J.," said Mrs. Claus. "I have a message for you from Santa, that we are coming for you tonight and I'm to let you know that your Canyon is not feeling well. Doctor K-9 thinks he just misses you and we all agree."

There was a silence on the telephone, then Aunty Joe said, "What time will you be arriving at the airfield?" Mrs. Claus said, "Our regular time." Then Aunty Joe said, "I will have Canyon's favourite meal ready for him to eat on the way back to the North Pole." The girls then went on to talk about other things that were going on at the North Pole.

Santa checked his watch as Mrs. Claus, Blinky and Canyon were getting into the sleigh, and it was time to go. Santa took the reins and snapped them, and as the jingles bells started to dance on the sides of Santa's reindeer, he yelled out, "Light the way, Rudolph! On Dasher, on Dancer, on Prancer, on Vixen, on Comet, on Cupid, on Donner and Blitzen." The reindeer pulled Santa's sleigh through the doors to the out-side, and a few seconds later, all four of them were on their way to pick up Aunty Joe. Canyon had put his head on Mrs. Claus' lap, where he fell fast asleep.

As the red sleigh cut through the air, Santa snapped the reins and the jingle bells rang in sync now as all of the reindeer went a little faster. Blinky was looking over the side of the sleigh to see the ground and the trees that were passing under the big red sleigh. Blinky was excited and it was great to be in Santa's sleigh. She had never been in Santa's sleigh and she had always wanted to ride in the back seat. Mrs. Claus looked in the back of the sleigh to see Blinky having her hand over the side of the sleigh like the wing of an airplane going up and down in the air. This put a smile on Mrs. Claus' face. She leaned over to tell Santa how much fun Blinky was having in the back of the sleigh. It did not take long to get from the North Pole to where Aunty Joe lived. As Santa put the sleigh into a circle over the landing field, Mrs. Claus and Blinky both spotted Aunty Joe at the same time in front of a lit sign. Aunty Joe was waving up to Santa, Mrs. Claus and Blinky.

Mrs. Claus and Blinky were waving and yelling, "Hello, Aunty Joe!" At that moment, Canyon woke up and sat up on the front seat as he started to look for Aunty Joe on the ground. He started to howl his favourite song, "Here Comes Santa, Here Comes Canyon, Right Down North Pole Lane" once he saw her waving up to him. Santa, Mrs. Claus and Blinky started to laugh as Santa lined up the sleigh for the final approach to the landing field. The sleigh started its descent and finally touched the ground. Santa pulled the reins back to stop the sleigh just behind the sign that Aunty Joe was standing next to.

Canyon jumped over Santa as if he was the tenth reindeer. Canyon hit the ground running and then was airborne again. He knocked Aunty Joe off her feet and was standing over her, licking her face and barking. Then Canyon stopped and looked up, as he could smell something in the air. He started to look around until he found it behind the sign. There was his favourite meal, and in a matter of a few seconds, the bowl was empty.

Santa looked at his watch; it was time to go. Aunty Joe, Blinky and Canyon got into the back of the sleigh and Santa and Mrs. Claus were in the front seat, where she sat right next to Santa. As Santa took the reins into both of his hands and was about to say the magic words to get the sleigh under way, when Mrs. Claus asked if she could fly them home. Santa just smiled and said, "Well, my dear, once you get your sleigh up to an nine-reindeer power, then I will let you fly my sleigh." Mrs. Claus moved away from sitting next to Santa and crossed her arms, looking away from Santa. Aunty Joe heard from some of the elves what had happened with Mrs. Claus' new sleigh and the castle.

Santa took the reins and yelled out, "Light the way, Rudolph! On Dasher, on Dancer, on Prancer, on Vixen, on Comet, on Cupid, on Donner and Blitzen." In a moment's notice, they were on their way back to the North Pole when Canyon's ears perked up as he looked towards the reindeer. The jingle bells were ringing Canyon's favourite song. So Aunty Joe, Blinky and Canyon started to sing "Here Comes Santa, Here Comes Canyon, Right Down North Pole Lane" and Santa and Mrs. Claus started to laugh.

Canyon Takes A Ride

```
B  Q  B  A  E  B  A  U  N  T  Y  J  O  E  S
L  C  A  N  L  V  Y  G  E  N  B  P  P  U  G
P  U  S  A  G  N  I  S  S  I  M  D  A  E  P
B  U  J  X  F  I  E  M  H  K  Y  L  L  L  P
V  A  K  M  R  Z  J  A  D  H  C  T  B  O  E
P  G  K  E  N  A  L  L  X  S  E  Z  I  P  E
Q  R  X  F  F  R  Z  A  R  R  Q  F  N  P  L
D  E  D  Q  Z  L  X  M  N  A  M  C  K  T  S
G  I  E  G  Q  D  H  U  Q  P  A  D  Y  R  A
E  N  B  N  X  C  X  T  D  N  E  U  Z  O  W
T  D  P  I  I  W  U  E  Y  E  L  L  I  N  G
V  E  J  V  D  Z  O  O  Z  K  U  C  C  L  U
N  E  J  A  Z  W  N  Q  S  A  N  T  A  X  I
I  R  Z  W  Q  O  Y  Q  S  V  P  J  S  P  Q
P  D  L  E  I  F  G  N  I  D  N  A  L  Z  C
G  C  S  E  N  O  H  P  E  L  E  T  S  G  S
T  Y  R  X  A  N  K  K  Q  M  M  D  G  N  N
```

MALAMUTE	BINKY	LANDING FIELD
TELEPHONE	REINDEER	WAVING
YELLING	NORTH POLE	CANYON
SANTA	MRS CLAUS	AUNTY JOE
ASLEEP	MISSING	LAP

CHAPTER 8

A Haircut for Santa

One morning, while Mrs. Claus and Santa were sitting across from each other, Mrs. Claus was watching Santa eat his breakfast. As he put another spoonful of cereal into his mouth, some milk and a few crumbs of cereal landed on Santa's beard. Mrs. Claus sat back in her chair to make sure she saw the next spoonful made it all the way into his mouth. Well, you can guess what happened – some milk hit his moustache and a few crumbs hit his beard again.

Well this would not do, as today was the day the family pictures were going to be taken. Santa was going to have to get his beard and moustache trimmed, and get a haircut as well. Mrs. Claus got up from the table and headed to the living room, where the phone was; she was going to call the barber to make an appointment for Santa.

After she made the appointment and came back into the kitchen, Santa was gone. Mrs. Claus started to search the castle for Santa; he was nowhere to be found. She went to the boot room only to find Santa's boots and snowsuit gone. Mrs. Claus started to move her head from left to right. "Well," Mrs. Claus thought, "Santa must be found for his barber appointment, but where to look?" So Mrs. Claus got ready to go outside.

She opened the back door to the castle, and as she stepped out, she noticed the bright, shiny red snowmobile was missing. Mrs. Claus thought, "Oh great, that man could be anywhere now!" Mrs. Claus went back into the castle to get her snowsuit, gloves and helmet.

As Mrs. Claus sat down on her snowmobile, she started it up and was about to go when the motor stopped. She turned the key one more time; the motor turned over, but it would not start. She looked at the gas gauge – it showed empty. Well, boys and girls, I bet you know what it's like when something does not go right for your dad and mom—are they happy? You guessed it! Mrs. Claus was not happy. She got off her snowmobile, grabbed the gas nozzle and stretched the hose from the pump, only to find it was six inches too short. All you could hear from Mrs. Claus' mouth was "Sugar shack and chocolate chip cookies!" She then went into the garage, looking for a jerry can to put just enough gas in to start the sled and get it closer to the pump, so she could fill it. Then she could go after Santa. Well, after a few minutes, Mrs. Claus could not find any jerry cans.

Mrs. Claus went back into the castle to find the keys for the snow cat. There was no way Santa was going to miss getting his hair cut today, and she was going to make sure of that. A few minutes later, with a set of keys in hand, she hopped into the snow cat and fired it up to check the gas gauge; it was full. Mrs. Claus pressed the accelerator down, and with the two levers in front of her to help steer, was on her way.

As she came around the corner, looking for Santa's tracks, she realized this was not going to be easy. She had to turn the windshield wipers on because it was snowing. But Mrs. Claus was a determined woman –Santa was going to get his hair cut today! Mrs. Claus stopped the snow cat for a moment, checking her watch to see what time it was; it was 7 a.m. Mrs. Claus pushed down on the accelerator pedal again; she knew exactly where she was going to go first. As the snow cat was plowing through the snow, her first stop was in sight. It was Jim's workshop. Jim was the young man that built Mrs. Claus' sled for her. Santa liked to visit Jim at least once a week. As the big snow cat pulled up in front of Jim's workshop, Mrs. Claus shut down the machine, then headed into Jim's workshop to see if Santa was there. Jim greeted Mrs. Claus at the door and Mrs. Claus asked Jim, "Have you seen Santa today?" Jim replied, "Why yes, Mrs. Claus, Santa was here. We had a cup of hot chocolate and then he said he must be on his way. There were a few places that he had to see before the family pictures for this year's Christmas cards." Mrs. Claus thanked Jim and then asked, "If you see Santa, please tell him to head back to the castle. There is a note on the fridge for him."

Mrs. Claus headed back to the snow cat to continue her journey. As the machine was running, Mrs. Claus looked around to see if she could see tracks from Santa's snowmobile. There were lots of tracks in the snow because the residents of Christmas Town were out and about doing their daily business, which made this a lot harder to find Santa. Mrs. Claus pushed down on the accelerator again, pulled the lever on the left side to turn left, then pushed the levers forward; the snow cat was on its way again. Mrs. Claus decided she would head to the kennel to see if Santa was there. He always like to bring treats for all the malamutes, especially Canyon. The kennel was not that far away. As Mrs. Claus pulled up to the kennel, she looked down to see a partial track from a snowmobile. She then thought, "Okay, he was here. Maybe Blinky will know where Santa went." Mrs. Claus shut the machine down once again, climbed out and headed for the front door of the kennel. It was bath day inside the kennel, and Blinky had Canyon in the bathtub. After his bath, he'd be heading for grooming. Mrs. Claus walked up behind Blinky. She then said, "Hello." This startled Blinky, and Canyon looked up at Mrs. Claus with a pair of sad brown eyes. Canyon did not like to have baths. Blinky stood up and took off one of her gloves to shake Mrs. Claus' hand. Mrs. Claus then asked Blinky, "Has Santa had been here today?" Blinky replied, "Yes, Santa has been here. He dropped off a bag of treats." Mrs. Claus asked Blinky, "Do you have any idea where Santa was off to next?" Blinky said, "Santa did mention he was going out to the Christmas tree forest and the cookie factory before family pictures for this year's Christmas card. Santa also said something about having to make a few more stops." Mrs. Claus thanked Blinky for giving her some leads in tracking down Santa. She then asked Blinky, "If you see Santa, please tell him to head back to the castle. There is a note on the fridge for him." Mrs. Claus thanked Blinky for all her help and hurried back to the snow cat. She had to hurry if she was going to catch up with Santa.

Mrs. Claus got herself comfortable in the snow cat. She turned on the radio to the song "Here Comes Santa Claus", and the first thing that crossed her mind was "hippity hop to the barbershop for Santa."

She started the snow cat and pushed the accelerator down. Lunging forward, Mrs. Claus was on her way at the whopping speed of 30km per hour, heading to the Christmas tree forest. This ride would've taken her almost an hour to get to the forest, but once she found Santa, she could get him to go on his snowmobile to the barbershop. As the snow cat plowed through the snow, the forest was soon within sight. As the snow cat was coming over the hill, Mrs. Claus saw snowmobile tracks. She then floored it, pushing the accelerator all the way down, thinking, "Come on, old girl. We've got to catch him."

Mrs. Claus finally made it to the gates of the forest. As she was getting out of the snow cat, there was a familiar noise. She realized, "Oh no, I've missed him!" She looked through the window to see Santa taking off in his snowmobile, heading back to Christmas Town. Well, the words that came out of Mrs. Claus' mouth were, "Oh, dang crumbled up Christmas paper!" She hopped back into the snow cat with keys in hand. Mrs. Claus pushed the accelerator all the way down to the floor. The diesel wound up as never before—there was a flame from the exhaust pipe and smoke was blowing black as coal! The snow cat lunged forward, her hands on the levers pushed forward. She knew she couldn't catch Santa, but she could follow his trail now. The snow had finally stopped coming down, which made it easier for Mrs. Claus to see snowmobile tracks.

Mrs. Claus then looked down at her gas gauge. She had half the tank fuel left; this would be just enough to get her back to Christmas Town. As Mrs. Claus was pulling into Christmas Town, she lost Santa's tracks once again, but Mrs. Claus knew that Santa was somewhere in Christmas Town and she was going to find him. Mrs. Claus looked down at her gas gauge once again to see it was running on empty, so she decided to go to North Pole Gas. As she pulled up next to the pump, the snow cat died. The elf attendant came out of the gas station to pump the diesel for Mrs. Claus. She asked the elf if he had seen Santa. The elf replied, "Yes, Mrs. Claus, he was here about 30 minutes ago. He gassed up his snowmobile and he headed towards the cookie factory, but I don't think he's there now. I did see him about fifteen minutes ago, heading back towards the castle." The nozzle clicked on the pump to say that the snow cat was now full. The elf took the nozzle out of the fuel tank, put the cap back on and put the nozzle back on the pump. Mrs. Claus paid for her fuel, then climbed back into the snow cat, put the key in the ignition and was about to start the snow cat when Santa went flying by. Mrs. Claus happened to look up to see the back of Santa's snowmobile heading towards the reindeer barn. Mrs. Claus was now in hot pursuit of

Santa! The reindeer barn was not far away from the gas station. It would take Mrs. Claus about 15 minutes to arrive at the barn. As she was pulling up, Santa's snowmobile was next to the barn; this put a smile on Mrs. Claus' face as she thought, "I have you now!"

She shut down the snow cat, climbed out and headed for Santa's snowmobile. She looked down to see the key was gone. Mrs. Claus headed inside the barn, only to find that Santa was not there, and his sled was missing. Mrs. Claus shook her head. She had forgotten today was the day that Santa takes the reindeer for a flight, just to give them exercise. He'd be gone for two hours. "Oh, crushed candy cane wrappers." Mrs. Claus looked at a couple of the elves and asked them to put a couple of reindeer together so she could use her sled to go after Santa. She then asked, "Do you know which way Santa went?" The elves looked at each other and said, "Mrs. Claus, no, we don't." The elves then hurried to get Mrs. Claus' sled ready for flight. It did not take the elves long and Mrs. Claus was airborne, looking for Santa and his sled.

Mrs. Claus started to wonder where to look. She snapped the reins on her sled and pointed Penny and Taz towards the village. Santa always like to head there, but she was not sure where he was going to fly next after the village. In a matter of moments, Mrs. Claus and her reindeer were over the village, and there was no sign of Santa and his sled. Both Penny and Taz looked towards the south and started pulling the sleigh in that direction. It did not take long for Mrs. Claus to understand why they were going that way. The sound of Santa's sleigh bells could be heard now off in the distance; this put a smile on Mrs. Claus' face. She looked down at her watch. There was still plenty of time to get back to Christmas Town and get Santa his haircut, so they could both have their pictures taken for this year's Christmas card. Mrs. Claus snapped the reins one more time, trying to get her reindeer to go just a little faster. In the distance, Mrs. Claus could see Santa's sled, and the sound coming from the jingle bells was getting louder. Mrs. Claus started to yell at Santa, but with the sound of the jingle bells, he could not hear her. He then made a turn, heading towards the Northwest Territories. "Oh no," Mrs. Claus thought. "He's going to take them out for a three-hour flight." Santa snapped his reins three times as Mrs. Claus watched Santa's sleigh disappear into some clouds.

Mrs. Claus followed into the clouds with her sleigh and her two reindeer, Penny and Taz. After searching for two hours and not finding Santa, Mrs. Claus headed back to the North Pole. She had had enough of this searching for Santa; she was going to wait for him back at the reindeer barn. Mrs. Claus pulled on the reins and headed back to the North Pole. She figured that she was about 45 minutes away from the North Pole. The young reindeer enjoyed pulling Mrs. Claus' sleigh and hoped that, one day, they could pull Santa's sleigh.

Christmas Town was now in sight and the reindeer barn was on the other side of the town. Mrs. Claus pulled back on the reins to slow down Penny and Taz, as the reindeer runway was in sight. Our young reindeer and our rookie pilot made a perfect landing. As the reindeer walked into the barn, Mrs. Claus noticed that Santa's sleigh was parked inside the barn. Mrs. Claus thought to herself, "Are you kidding me?" Once she had stopped her sleigh, she looked over at the elves and then asked, "When did Santa return, and did you tell him that I was looking for him?" One of the elves spoke up and said, "Santa was in an awful hurry and said he'd come back here later to find out where you had gone. We did not get a chance to tell him what you had said." Mrs. Claus then said, "Sugar shack! Oh, dagnabit and hanging mistletoe." She snapped her fingers. Mrs. Claus then climbed down from her sled and headed to say thank you to Penny and Taz by rubbing them along the side of the face. She had to go.

As she was leaving, she turned to the elves and asked, "Do you by chance know where Santa is going?" All the elves looked at her and all but one shook their heads and said "No." The one elf said, "I saw Santa heading back to Christmas Town on his snowmobile." Mrs. Claus thanked the young elf and headed back to the snow cat; it fired back up with no problem. Mrs. Claus backed the snow cat up, pulled the right lever towards her and pushed the left one forward, and the snow cat turned on a dime. She then pushed the right lever forward all the way, and once again was heading back to Christmas Town, looking for Santa. Mrs. Claus looked at her watch. It was almost time for the pictures. She decided to head back to the castle to get changed and wait for the photographer and Santa.

As she was pulling up to the front of the castle, Hannah was just pulling up with her team of Alaskan malamutes. Mrs. Claus was a little envious of Hannah's dog team; it brought back memories of when she had her own team and sled. Mrs. Claus shut the snow cat down and put a smile on her face to greet Hannah. As the two girls were talking and walking into the castle, Santa was standing in front of the doorway with his best red suit on. His beard and moustache were trimmed nicely and he had got his hair cut. Hannah said, "Oh, Santa, you look so dapper!" Santa reached for his hat, removed it, bowed in front of Hannah and Mrs. Claus and said, "Why thank you, my dear." Santa then put his hat back on his head. Mrs. Claus said, "Oh Santa, you and I will have to have a little chat later tonight." Santa started to laugh and said, "Of course, my dear," then a very loud "Ho, Ho, Ho" came out of Santa.

Merry Christmas!

From Santa and Mrs. Claus

Mrs Claus is looking high and low for Santa.
Follow her in the hunt for Santa.

A Haircut For Santa

```
B  L  O  P  K  G  U  S  A  T  C  S  P  F  H
D  L  N  B  P  T  E  A  L  W  K  E  O  E  K
E  W  G  H  H  T  H  N  A  M  U  S  H  R  A
G  F  F  T  H  D  M  T  S  P  A  I  S  B  K
A  K  U  N  Y  E  K  A  K  L  W  C  R  R  W
L  D  Q  J  F  J  F  S  A  W  E  R  E  G  K
L  H  R  W  S  A  U  L  N  L  U  E  B  O  O
I  V  Z  K  E  N  N  E  L  F  V  X  R  M  U
V  P  T  P  N  F  L  I  G  H  T  E  A  Q  U
I  W  R  A  E  D  Q  G  R  O  I  U  B  U  V
C  N  D  A  E  O  F  H  K  H  Z  X  N  T  Q
J  D  R  S  J  I  N  G  L  E  B  E  L  L  S
G  S  N  I  E  R  M  B  W  G  D  F  U  C  A
P  H  O  T  O  G  R  A  P  H  V  G  J  W  Z
H  Z  O  U  L  S  U  G  A  R  S  H  A  C  K
B  Z  T  Q  L  R  N  R  F  G  W  E  G  O  B
N  I  M  I  S  S  I  N  G  N  I  K  O  O  L
```

BARBERSHOP	MISSING	SUGAR SHACK
EXERCISE	FLIGHT	VILLAGE
DEAR	PHOTOGRAPH	ALASKAN
JINGLE BELLS	REINS	SANTA SLEIGH
LOOKING	KEY	KENNEL

Robin White

CHAPTER 9

Homemade Christmas Cookie

Donna Northern Lights was reaching into her purse to pull out a key to open her office door. The phone was ringing on her desk. She hurried over to her desk to pick up the telephone receiver and said, "Hello?" On the other end of the telephone was Jennifer Searcher, and she responded by saying, "Hi, Donna! What are you up to and how would you like to go for a quick hot chocolate at that new hot chocolate store next to my office at the tracking centre?" Donna replied, "Sure, I will meet you at the hot chocolate shop in ten minutes."

Meanwhile, up at the castle, Santa was sitting in his favourite chair in the bedroom and he could smell all the food cooking from the kitchen; every smell was fantastic. Christmas Cookie was laying on Santa's lap. She was licking her paws as Santa was petting her. He noticed she was a little lighter in weight as he picked her up to put her on the floor. Christmas Cookie walked towards the hearth of the fireplace, where a fire was lit. Christmas Cookie laid down on her pillow what was in front of the fireplace.

Christmas Cookie did not have a care in the world at this moment. Santa started to read a book called Santa's Christmas Memoirs Volume One. As Santa was reading, his eyelids were starting to get heavy. Santa was about to go to sleep in dreamland when he heard a cat crying and calling out for Christmas Cookie. Santa woke up from a dead sleep and looked towards the pillow that was on the floor, to see Christmas Cookie was also sound asleep and dreaming; her legs and head were moving, and she was crying in her sleep as well. Her back was facing the warmth that was coming from the fireplace.

Santa got out of his chair and walked towards the fireplace. He stopped at the wood box and picked up couple pieces of wood to put into the fireplace to keep the bedroom nice and warm. Santa looked down at Christmas Cookie on her pillow. At that moment, this startled Christmas Cookie from her sleep and woke her up; she looked up at Santa. As he was opening the glass door to the fireplace to put the piece of wood into the firebox, Christmas Cookie got off her pillow and walked towards Santa, rubbed her body on his right leg, then headed towards the bedroom window to look out at all the homes of Christmas Town.

Santa watched as Christmas Cookie jumped onto the ledge and Santa started to wonder, "Where did you come from, Christmas Cookie? From where did you catch a ride on my sleigh?" Christmas Cookie was looking for a very special person that saved her from that monster of a dog.

Santa walked towards the telephone that was on his side of the bed. He picked up the telephone receiver and called down to the kitchen. He wanted to talk to Dexter about Christmas Cookie.

As the telephone was ringing in the kitchen, Christmas Cookie was looking out the window towards Christmas Town to see all the elves going about their daily lives and jobs. Christmas Cookie's tail was swinging back and forth as if she was looking for someone or something. The red snow cat pulled up to the front of the castle and stopped at the front doors; Christmas Cookie looked down towards the driver's side of the snow cat as the door opened.

Back at the hot chocolate shop, Donna and Jennifer met at the front door at the same time. They both entered the hot chocolate shop and headed for the counter to order an extra-large double double hot chocolate and two boxes of doughnuts each. After they collected their orders, the girls found a table in the corner and started to chat. As they were talking, Donna asked, "Jennifer, you remember the last Santa challenge we had at the North Pole?" Jennifer was picking up her hot chocolate and was about to take a drink but stopped. Jennifer put her hot chocolate cup back onto the table. She sat back in her chair and said, "Do you know, Donna, I can't remember when we had the last Santa challenge here at the North Pole."

Donna's e-pad (Elf Pad) started to vibrate while it was laying on the table. Both girls look down at the e-pad—it was a message from Santa, wondering what events he and Mrs. Claus had to attend today.

As Donna was reading the message, Jennifer looked at her watch. It was time for her to go to work. Jennifer headed back to the counter to order another extra-large double double. Both of them said goodbye. Donna responded to Santa's message, "Hello, Santa. I just checked my booking calendar for you and Mrs. Claus, and you both have a day off. I am on my way back to the castle. See you in a few moments."

Christmas Cookie spotted Mrs. Claus climbing out of her snow cat and heading to the front door of the castle. This was normally Christmas Cookie's cue to head to the front door and meet Mom, as she had done every day since she arrived to live with the Clauses. However, today there was something different with Christmas Cookie, as if she was sick, because as soon at the door to the bedroom opened, she usually flew out the door between Santa's feet to meet Mom. But not today. Christmas Cookie walked very slowly next to Santa, as they both headed for the front door. Santa wanted to talk to Mrs. Claus about Christmas Cookie; he wanted to know if she was okay. Santa was going to call Doctor K-9 to come and check Christmas Cookie, but Santa wanted to check with Mrs. Claus first.

As the two were heading to the front door, Dexter beat both of them. He had one of the giant oak doors open for Mrs. Claus as she approached the door. She was taking off her coat to hand to Dexter. Dexter held out his arm and said, "Hello, Mrs. Claus. How was your day at the office?" Mrs. Claus responded, "I had a very nice day, and thank you for asking, Dexter. How was my little girl today, and how much trouble did she get into?" Dexter answered Mrs. Claus' question, "Well, Mrs. Claus, Christmas Cookie stayed on her pillow most of the day. She came down to the kitchen only once. She had her lunch and some water, then she headed back upstairs. Oh, here she comes now with Santa." Mrs. Claus looked towards the stairs to see Christmas Cookie walking right next to Santa coming down the stairs. Mrs. Claus walked towards them both.

Santa held out his arms as Mrs. Claus approached him. After they were done hugging each other, Mrs. Claus looked down towards Christmas Cookie. Mrs. Claus bent towards her girl and picked her up to give her a hug as well. Christmas Cookie wrapped her little arms around Mrs. Claus' neck, pushed her little head along the left side of Mrs. Claus' cheek and let out a soft cry. This was the first time she had done that. Mrs. Claus held Christmas Cookie a little tighter and said, "What's the matter, my girl? You are safe and okay, my baby girl." There was a little tear coming down the right side of Christmas Cookie's nose. Mrs. Claus could feel the little hug was a bit tighter than normal. Mrs. Claus then started to pat Christmas Cookie on her back very gently. Mrs. Claus looked at Santa and said, "Santa, I think our little girl is sick. I will take her over to see Doctor K-9 and maybe he can find out with is the matter with our baby girl?"

Santa looked at his wife and said, "Yes, my dear, we will take her over right now!" Santa then looked over at Dexter and asked him, "Dexter, can you call the hospital and get a hold of old Doctor K-9; let him know we are on our way with Christmas Cookie and that we are not sure what is wrong with her?" Dexter replied, "Yes, Santa and Mrs. Claus, you both better hurry with our Christmas Cookie and get her well right away!"

At that moment, Donna Northern Lights came around the corner; she was the Clauses' personal secretary for all the events that happened at the North Pole. Santa saw Donna first. Santa asked, "Donna, can you get Christmas Cookie's carrier? We need to take her to see Doctor K-9." Donna replied, "Yes, Santa, I will let the hospital know you have an animal emergency and you and Mrs. Claus are en route!" Before anyone could say or do anything, Donna hit a button on her Bluetooth earpiece to get a hold of the hospital and was on her way to get Christmas Cookie's cat carrier.

In a flash, Donna was back as if she was wearing roller skates on her elf boots, with a green cat carrier and a very warm blanket inside to keep Christmas Cookie nice and warm. Dexter went and got both Clauses' long coats.

Dexter opened the big oak front doors for the emergency run to the hospital. The Clauses were off; Santa carried the carrier, and with his free hand, he opened the passenger door to the snow cat for Mrs. Claus. Once she was in her seat and buckled in, Santa handed the carrier to Mrs. Claus. Santa then closed the passenger door to the snow cat. He hurried to the driver's side and started the snow cat up, and they were on their way to the hospital.

As the Clauses were pulling away from the front of the castle,

Donna was on the phone again, calling traffic control. The phone stopped ringing and there was a voice on the other end, "Hello, North Pole Emergency Control Centre, Ruben Christmas Lights here, state the nature of your emergency?" Donna answered, "Hello Ruben, this is Donna Northern Lights, and I'm the Clauses' personal secretary. I am calling to let you know that we have had an emergency at the castle; the Clauses are on their way to the hospital. We need to activate the North Pole emergency program in test mode! Can you make sure all the traffic lights are on green mode all the way to the hospital for Santa and Mrs. Claus?" Ruben said, "Yes, we can active the North Pole emergency program in test mode!" Ruben and Donna said thank you and goodbye to each other.

Ruben hung up the telephone, then called everyone on the emergency services list, saying, "We have a North Pole emergency test mode running to the North Pole Hospital! You are looking for Mrs. Claus' red snow cat. They are just leaving the castle now!" Ruben turned his chair to the left and placed his hands on the keyboard to send a live message to all of the North Pole emergency vehicles' computer screens as well. Ruben, at that moment, looked up at his television monitors that are hooked to all the street traffic lights, and spotted Mrs. Claus' red snow cat coming down driveway to the entrance to street. There was a traffic camera there, pointing at the first traffic light; like Christmas magic, the lights started to change to green for Christmas Cookie's run to the hospital.

Christmas Cookie was looking through the wire gate of her cat carrier and she was wondering what all the excitement was about. Christmas Cookie could hear the sirens of the police snowmobile coming closer and closer to the snow cat. Christmas Cookie headed to the back of the cat carrier; her little tummy was scared, and she went to hide in her warm blankets. She thought this did not sound good for Mrs. Claus.

Mrs. Claus was looking out the front windshield to see two police elf officers on their snowmobiles with their emergency lights and sirens on. She looked out her passenger door of her snow cat to see two more police elf officers on their snowmobiles with their emergency lights and sirens on. They were getting an escort! She looked at Santa and said, "Santa, what is going on? Why are we getting a police elf escort, and why are all the lights green now? What is going on?" Santa had a bit of a smile on his face, but never thought he would ever use the emergency program at the North Pole.

Santa stepped on the gas pedal of the snow cat and the tracks of the snow cat dug into the hardened snow. Santa looked at his driver's side mirror to see a four-foot rooster tail of snow coming off the snow cat tracks, and the Clauses were pushed back into their seats.

Santa then said, "Well, my dear, a few months ago, our North Pole IT guy, Marcus Von Reindeer, came to me and asked if he could install this system to help the citizens of Christmas Town. When someone calls 9-1-1 or the North Pole Emergency Control Centre to let them know that there is an emergency, everything is put into play to help. You are now seeing it first-hand, in action. How do you like this system? I know everyone wanted to test this system with us; well, today is test day, I guess. Oh yes, hang on Mrs. Claus, we have to turn this corner." Santa started to turn the big snow cat.

As the snow cat started to turn left at the corner, the engine started to rev a little louder. Mrs. Claus now looked out of the passenger window to see a blue North Pole sky. Her snow cat was only on one track; she grabbed the handhold, as well as hanging on to the cat carrier, then there was a loud bang as the right side of the snow cat as the track hit the hardened snow. Santa and Mrs. Claus bounced in their seats and so did Christmas Cookie in her cat carrier. Santa then asked, "Mrs. Claus, what did you do to this snow cat?" They made the corner that lead to the driveway to the hospital. Mrs. Claus was looking out the front window to see Doctor K-9 and three nurses waiting with a stretcher for the emergency to arrive.

Santa started to slow the snow cat down and then stopped. Santa hurried to open Mrs. Claus' door, but Doctor K-9 beat him, and Mrs. Claus handed the cat carrier to Doctor K-9. The doctor placed the cat carrier on the stretcher and the nurses rushed Christmas Cookie into the emergency room. Mrs. Claus was right behind her girl. Santa went to talk to all of the people who helped them get to the hospital in great time, and he thanked each and every one of them that was at the hospital with a handshake; he would go and thank the crew at the traffic control centre later on.

At that moment, the media showed up. Donna was already there to answer any questions regarding this test of the new North Pole emergency program. After Donna had finished dealing with Mr. Fred Newsprint, a reporter from Aunty Joe's Christmas newsroom, she headed towards Santa and asked, "Santa, is there was anything else that needs to be done?" Santa replied, "No, Donna, tomorrow we can send out our thank you letters to everyone involved in the emergency program. As well, a letter of thank you for every one that worked today." Donna was writing every word that Santa had said. Santa and Donna headed into the hospital.

Mrs. Claus was in the emergency room with Christmas Cookie and the hospital staff. The emergency staff were talking amongst themselves on how the test went on their part. Doctor K-9 was more concerned with his young patient; he had ordered a lot of medical tests. As the tests were being run, Santa was sitting next to Mrs. Claus, holding her hand. With his other hand, he was patting the top of the hand he was holding. Every once in a while, they heard a nurse scream in pain—this told the Clauses that Christmas Cookie was still putting up a fight.

Christmas Cookie did not like this place at all! She wanted her nice, soft red pillow that was next to the fireplace in the Clauses' bedroom, or her pillow in the living room. Doctor K-9 was talking with Mrs. Claus about Christmas Cookie when the sound of another nurse feeling the wrath of Christmas Cookie's claws was heard. Doctor K-9 stopped talking to Mrs. Claus and looked towards the examining room, where Christmas Cookie was with all the nurses and medical techs.

Santa asked, "Doctor K-9, when will you know what is wrong with our little girl?" Mrs. Claus decided to head into the examining room to be with her baby girl. The doctor replied, "Santa, we are almost done our tests, if I don't run out of nurses first!" Santa tried not to laugh at the doctor's comment. Santa was about to ask another question when the sound of Mrs. Claus' voice could be heard coming from the examining room saying, "Christmas Cookie, what are you doing, young lady? You be nice to these nurses and to Doctor K-9!"

Christmas Cookie had another nurse in her sights. There was a very loud cry heard from a defiant and sassy Christmas Cookie as she sat in her cage, looking through the bars at Mrs. Claus. The only thing that was missing was a tin cup being raked across the bars of her cage and someone playing a song on the harmonica from another pet cell across from Christmas Cookie's cage. Mrs. Claus looked at Christmas Cookie and thought, "How sassy you are right now, young lady!"

At that moment, Santa and Doctor K-9 entered the emergency treatment room. The nurse approached Doctor K-9 with all the lab reports and handed them to the doctor. Santa looked over at the stack of reports that the doctor was holding and reading. Doctor K-9 had a funny look on his face as he finished reading the reports. He put his right hand behind his head and started to scratch it. He looked over at Christmas Cookie's cage and then said, "Santa and Mrs. Claus, can we go into the waiting room? I have some things to tell you." Mrs. Claus and Santa looked at each other and they followed Doctor K-9 out to the waiting room.

Doctor K-9 was about tell the Clauses the findings of the reports. The only thing they could find wrong with Christmas Cookie was that she had lost some weight and some hair. Doctor K-9 asked, "Santa, where did you find her?" Santa replied, "Doctor, I have no idea where she caught a ride. The last place was an old apartment building in Canada, which was the only time the sleigh was left alone for a few minutes." Doctor K-9 looked back at the chart for a few seconds, then he took off his glasses, folded his arms and tapped the rim of his glasses on his lower lip. Doctor K-9 said, "Well, Mrs. Claus, your little girl is sick, but not in a bad way, she is homesick." Mrs. Claus looked at Santa and then back at Doctor K-9. She was at a loss for words.

Santa said, "Well, I am going to go and find out where she came from, right now!" Santa headed outside and picked up a handful of snow and made it into a snowball; he looked inside it to see a baby Christmas Cookie. As Santa was watching inside the snowball, he could see two other cats on that old apartment rooftop, looking for their baby girl after Santa had left, heading for his next city in Canada. Santa had to pick up another snowball to see in present time, that Christmas Cookie's parents were still looking for her. After seeing this, Santa knew he had to go and tell Mrs. Claus that they had to take Christmas Cookie home to her family, and if she and her family wanted to come to the North Pole, they would be welcome.

Santa put the snowball down and headed back to where Mrs. Claus and Doctor K-9 were standing, watching Santa looking into the snowballs to see where Christmas Cookie came from. Santa entered the hospital and said, "Well, Mrs. Claus, we are heading to Dawson Creek, Canada, to an apartment building where Christmas Cookie got on my sleigh." Santa stopped speaking. He looked at Mrs. Claus, then said, "Mrs. Claus, my reindeer have not recovered from our last trip, do you think your new sleigh, and Taz and Penny, can give us a ride to Dawson Creek and back to the North Pole?"

Mrs. Claus said, "Why, yes!" She had a very large smile on her face, and she did a fist pump into the air and said, "Yesss!" Doctor K-9 started to laugh. Santa went to the front desk of the hospital, called the reindeer barn and talked to Kelly, the head elf of the reindeer barn. Kelly picked up the receiver to answer the phone in his office, "Hello, reindeer barn, Kelly here, how can I help you?" Then Kelly took a breath to hear who was on the other end. Santa said, "Hello, Kelly, I need you to hook up Taz and Penny to Mrs. Claus' sleigh. We are going for a short trip to Dawson Creek in British Columbia, Canada." Santa stopped and waited for Kelly to answer.

Kelly looked at the phone, then looked up to see Wally had come into his office now. Kelly responded, "Santa, would you like Wally to go with you as well?" Santa said, "No, thank you. It will be just Mrs. Claus and myself going on this fast trip. We will be leaving in 30 minutes." Santa then said, "I want the jingle bells put on these two reindeer harnesses—they deserve it after their last flight!" Then they said goodbye to each other. They both hung up the receivers. Kelly looked Wally's way and told him what Santa wanted.

Santa headed back to where Mrs. Claus and Doctor K-9 were standing and said, "We are going to go and take her home to where her parents are still looking for her. We will offer them a chance to live at the North Pole with us."

Mrs. Claus said, "Oh, Santa, we will need to call the kitchen and get a lunch made for all of us and extra food for Christmas Cookie's family for their trip back to the North Pole." Mrs. Claus went to the front desk to call the castle. Donna was still sitting in the front lobby of the hospital, waiting for word on how Christmas Cookie was doing, when Mrs. Claus spotted Donna and headed towards her. Donna asked, "How is Christmas Cookie doing, Mrs. Claus?" Mrs. Claus replied, "She is going to be fine. The doctor thinks she is homesick and missing her parents, so we are going to Dawson Creek to ask her family to come and live here at the North Pole with us and Christmas Cookie. We hope they will accept."

Mrs. Claus then said, "Donna, I need you to get a hold of the kitchen and Dexter to let them know we need lunches made, and warmer clothing as well an extra cat carrier, just in case."

Donna wrote this all down in her e-pad and then quickly sent an email to the castle and reindeer barn. This put a smile on Donna's face, and then Donna wondered how Dexter was going to like this—a few more permanent guests at the castle.

Donna's e-pad started to ding as emails came in from the castle and the reindeer barn; they would be ready to go. Donna read the messages as she was walking towards Santa. Donna was standing in front of Santa and Mrs. Claus; she cleared her throat and both the Clauses looked towards the elf. Santa said, "Yes, Donna?" Donna replied, "Santa, I have advised all of the parties that needed to know about your trip to the south. The reindeer barn said everything is ready to go for your flight, and the kitchen has made some meals and packed extra food for our new guests. Dexter has all of the winter gear on its way to the reindeer barn, and it will be loaded into Mrs. Claus' sleigh."

Doctor K-9 came out of the examination room carrying Christmas Cookie's cat carrier with her inside of it, and Santa thanked the doctor and his fine staff for the great job they did with the tests and taking care of their little girl. Mrs. Claus also thanked Doctor K-9, and she was very sorry for any pain that Christmas Cookie caused his medical staff.

Santa said, "Well, Mrs. Claus, I think it's time we made our little girl happy. We have a long flight with only two-reindeer power." This put a smile on Santa's face. Santa shook Doctor K-9's hand and the Clauses were out the emergency door and headed to the snow cat. Santa started the snow cat's motor. He opened the driver's door of the snow cat and called Donna over. Donna approached the driver's side of the snow cat to find out what Santa wanted.

Santa said, "Donna, can you contact Jennifer at the tracking centre and let her know that Santa Sleigh Two is heading to Dawson Creek, British Columbia, Canada. We will be leaving in 20 minutes and returning in the morning. Have Doctor K-9 at the reindeer barn just in case our new guests may need his help." Donna was writing this all down on her e-pad and sending the request out, then she would call them to make sure they were aware of what was about to happen at the North Pole. Donna said, "Okay, Santa, is there anything else I need to know or do to make this flight a go?" Santa looked at Mrs. Claus, then back towards Donna and said, "No, Donna, that is all I can think of for the moment, but we better get going so we can get back. Okay, Donna, bye for now!" Santa then closed the driver's door and put the snow cat into gear; the three of them were off to the reindeer barn and then to Dawson Creek.

As the snow cat was pulling up to the reindeer barn, Mrs. Claus saw her new sleigh for the first time since her accident; Santa had it painted bright red to match her dress and long coat. Wally walked up to the passenger door to the snow cat to let out Mrs. Claus and to take the cat carrier that had Christmas Cookie inside of it. Wally took the carrier to Santa Sleigh Two. Mrs. Claus had carrots and apple slices for Penny and Taz. As Santa approached the two young reindeer, they both looked over at him and stood up straight, as if someone had yelled "Attention!"

Both Penny and Taz thought that this was their chance to fly with Santa at the reins and show him what they could do. As they were about to take off, Kelly ordered the jingle bells to be attached to the two reindeers' harnesses. As the bells were being attached, both Taz and Penny had gingerbread men dancing in their stomachs. Mrs. Claus had the reins in her hands; both Taz and Penny looked back at this, and they put their heads down in disappointment. Mrs. Claus noticed that, so she handed the reins of her reindeer to Santa.

Santa was happy to take the reins. He looked at Mrs. Claus and said, "My dear, can you say the magic words that get your reindeer on their way?" Mrs. Claus said in a nice, clear voice, "Okay Taz, okay Penny, it's time to up, up and away! Fly, fly away!" There was a slight jerk on the reins—Mrs. Claus' sleigh was being pulled down the runway, slowly at first, then it started to gain speed, and the next moment, Santa, Mrs. Claus, Taz and Penny were off the ground with Santa Sleigh Two being pulled into the evening sky. Christmas Cookie was sitting in between the Clauses; she did not like the wind coming into her cat carrier. Christmas Cookie was happy that Dexter put two extra blankets in her carrier. She stood up in the carrier and started to walk in a circle, trying to find that sweet spot and then bury herself in the two blankets so she could keep warm.

Mrs. Claus reached into the back of her sleigh and grabbed a blanket to put over her legs, and the carrier as well. Santa was looking down at the two-way radio that was under the dashboard. The radio was not on. He looked over at Mrs. Claus and asked, "Hey, my Christmas stocking, can you turn on the two-way radio so Jennifer at the tracking centre can keep an eye on us? Please and thank you." Santa gave her a wink with his right eye. Santa then looked up at the stars to see where they were.

A green light appeared on Jennifer's tracking board on the wall. Jennifer took the microphone in her right hand and pressed down on the transmit key and called to Santa Sleigh Two to do a radio check. Jennifer said, "North Pole tracking centre to Santa Sleigh Two, do you copy?" Jennifer moved to her keyboard to update who was on the sleigh to put into the flight log. The sound of static could be heard in the speakers at the tracking centre. Then a woman's voice came on the air and said, "Hello, Jennifer, this is Santa Sleigh Two checking in. We have the following on board: Santa, Christmas Cookie and me are heading to Dawson Creek, British Columbia, Canada." Mrs. Claus released the microphone key. Jennifer replied, "Hello, Mrs. C, thank you for the update. We hope all three of you have a safe trip. This is Jennifer out."

Mrs. Claus put the microphone back on its hanger on the dashboard. As she was looking towards Santa, she said, "Do you know, Santa, that Jennifer is a nice girl and a hard worker as well." Santa looked over at his wife and nodded his head in agreement. Santa wanted to test both Penny and Taz on some drills that a reindeer must know when flying with Santa on December 24th. Santa was very impressed how Taz and Penny reacted to pulling Mrs. Claus' sleigh.

Mrs. Claus decided to check on Christmas Cookie; she was sound asleep, rolled up inside the blankets in her cat carrier. Suddenly, Mrs. Claus started to think, "What if Christmas Cookie does not want to live at the North Pole?" Mrs. Claus did not want to think about that, but what if Christmas Cookie wanted to stay with her family in Canada? Santa happened to look over at his wife to see she was crying; he knew she must have been thinking about if Christmas Cookie wanted to stay with her family. "Well," he thought to himself, "that is one snow bridge we will have to cross when it comes."

Mrs. Claus wiped her cheek and asked, "Santa, would you like some hot chocolate to warm you up?" Santa smiled at Mrs. Claus and replied, "Sure, my dear, as long as you have a cup with me." Mrs. Claus smiled and reached into the back of her sleigh and pulled the thermos out of the red bag that Dexter had sent to the North Pole reindeer barn for their trip.

As the five travellers were heading south, not much was being said. The only sound that was heard was the jingle bells ringing in the air and around Santa Sleigh Two. Santa looked up at the stars in the sky to see they were approaching the corner of Yukon and British Columbia in Canada. Santa started to slow the young reindeer down, because he was not sure how they were at approaching a landing area, so he wanted to give them a little extra room to land safely. Santa spotted the apartment as the sleigh approached from the north.

Taz and Penny were still a bit nervous about their first landing with Santa at the reins, when Penny whispered over to Taz and asked, "Tazie, I don't remember how to land!" Taz looked over at Penny with a shocked look! Then Taz replied, "Don't worry, Pen, just watch me and I will get you and the Clauses and Christmas Cookie down, nice and safe." Then Taz winked at Penny. Penny started to breathe a little easier and she felt a little stronger inside, knowing that Taz and she could do this for Mrs. Claus. They were now five feet off the ground and getting lower every second until they touched down. The young reindeer hooves were on the roof, and the sleigh runners were now sliding a couple of feet, and they all stopped at the same time. After they stopped, Mrs. Claus said, "Way to go, Penny and Taz, we knew you could do this! Right, Santa?" Santa had a smile on his face and said, "Yes. Mrs. Claus, Christmas Cookie and myself all knew that you could do it and you both did a great job, I must say!" This put a smile on each reindeer face.

Well, it was now time to find Christmas Cookie's family. Santa got out of the sleigh first and he walked around from the back of the sleigh to Mrs. Claus' side. He put his hand out to help her. Once she was out and both her boots were on the roof of the building, Santa gave his bride of so many years a hug and a kiss on the cheek. Santa asked, "Mrs. C, are you okay?" Mrs. Claus had her head bowed. She then looked up into her husband's eyes to see love and care beaming towards hers, and Mrs. Claus could not find the right words right at that moment. She gave Santa an even bigger hug for a few moments. Santa gave his best girl a hug back, then he took her by the hand. With his free hand, he reached into the sleigh and grabbed the cat carrier off the front seat of Santa Sleigh Two so he could pass it to Mrs. Claus. Santa knew that she would want to carry the cat carrier with Christmas Cookie inside back to her family. There was a sadness in Mrs. Claus' heart at the thought of losing her baby girl. Santa took Mrs. Claus' right hand, as they stood next to the chimney of the apartment where Christmas Cookie had caught a ride to the North Pole.

Santa looked at Christmas Cookie through the bars of her cage. She was looking out as if to say, "I have been here before." Still hanging onto Mrs. Claus' hand, he put his right finger alongside his nose, and down the chimney the three of them flew. The next thing Mrs. Claus and Christmas Cookie knew, they were in an empty apartment. Mrs. Claus bent down with the cat carrier and opened the door to the cage. Christmas Cookie slowly came out of the cage; she stopped halfway out and started to look around the empty apartment. The moon was full outside—the light was beaming into the front room through the patio doors. Christmas Cookie was all the way out of her cage now, and she was sniffing the air in the apartment.

She sat in the middle of the living room floor and looked back at Mrs. Claus as if to ask, "What happened here?" Christmas Cookie let out a cry for a few seconds, then headed back to her cat carrier. As she was halfway into the carrier, she stopped and backed out, as if she was listening to something. She let out another cry. This time, both Clauses heard it as well. It was a cry coming through the furnace vents. Santa looked at Mrs. Claus and said, "My dear, you need to put Christmas Cookie back in her cage, so we can go to the sound of those cries."

In a flash, all three were in the basement. They looked around to see an old, dark grey furnace in the middle of the room; the walls were unpainted cement with a few spider webs in the corners and had some empty wooden shelves on the north wall. Hanging from the ceiling was a 30-watt lightbulb that gave off a low light in the basement. Next to the door, on the south wall in the corner, was an old army cot and an empty toilet paper box on its side with an old blanket inside of it.

Mrs. Claus put the carrier down and opened it again. This time, Christmas Cookie came flying out of the cage to see the old army cot in the corner. Outside of the box were two empty dishes. Christmas Cookie looked into the box to see two small animals looking towards Mrs. Claus, Santa and Christmas Cookie. Christmas Cookie walked towards the box as if she knew who was in there. She stopped a few feet from the front of the box and started to sniff the air, then gave a very soft cry. There was no answer from the box. Christmas Cookie tried one more time.

This time, there was an answer. Christmas Cookie knew whose voice it was. Christmas Cookie let out a loud meow back to answer. A black cat came slowly out of the box, his back was arched and his tail was big and fluffy. The Clauses looked at the box to see a white cat coming out. She was staring at this black-and-white cat in their home, and how dare she! Then Santa let out a "Ho, ho, ho!" and all three cats stopped and looked towards Santa. Mrs. Claus went down on one knee and called out, "Christmas Cookie, come here!" Christmas Cookie turned her head and turned it back. Christmas Cookie did not move, she was going to stand her ground.

The white cat approached Christmas Cookie. She was a long-haired white cat with blue eyes; her name was Lacey. Lacey was now close enough to smell Christmas Cookie, and she smelled like a house cat. Lacey looked down at Christmas Cookie's feet to see that she had extra toes on all four of her paws. Lacey knew who this was now—it was their daughter! She had gone missing last Christmas Eve. Lacey looked towards the black cat with short hair. Lacey let Joshua know to stand down, "This is our baby girl!" Joshua walked towards Christmas Cookie, and he started to lick her forehead like the way he used to do when she was a kitten. Joshua then walked over to Santa and rubbed up against his right leg. Joshua sat down in front of Santa and looked up into Santa's face. At that moment, Joshua knew that he and his wife Lacey were safe with these two people.

Santa went down on one knee and started to pet Joshua, then Santa said, "Hello, Joshua and Lacey. As you can see, we took good care of your little girl. My wife, Mrs. Claus, and I would like to invite you all to come and join our family at the North Pole."

At that moment, Christmas Cookie started to meow at her parents. She walked to the cage and went in and came back out. She did this a few times. Lacey walked over to her husband and stood by him. Joshua rubbed his head on Lacey's head; they did that for a few seconds, and they both looked around the basement room they were living in. The basement door opened, to the surprise of the Clauses and Christmas Cookie. An old man walked into the basement, and he was holding a bowl of water in one hand. In his other hand, he had some wet food. The old man came into the basement room and the first thing he saw on the basement floor was Christmas Cookie, looking right at him. The old man said, "Well, who are you and where did you come from?"

Lacey started to meow and walk around Christmas Cookie, as if to protect her. The old man put the bowl of water and the plate of food down side-by-side on the basement floor. The old man did not see the Clauses, who were hiding behind the furnace, watching and listening to the old man speak to the three cats. "Well, Joshua, Lacey, we are going to have to move; the people that own this building say I can't keep you."

The old man sat on his bed and started to cry into his hands. He did not know what to do. The owners of the building were looking for a younger person to take over his job. As the old man was talking to Joshua, Lacey and this new kitten, Santa and Mrs. Claus were listening to what the old man had to say from behind the furnace. Mrs. Claus looked at Santa and she could not believe what she was hearing. Well, Christmas Cookie had had enough of this; she went to get Mrs. Claus. She and her husband could help this person, Christmas Cookie knew they could. "Then all of us will be off back home," Christmas Cookie thought. Well, she stopped in front of Mrs. Claus, and she started to meow and meow. She would not stop until the old man stopped crying and got off his bed; he walked to the furnace to see the Clauses standing there. The look on his face was one of shock and disbelief.

Santa came out from behind the furnace to say hello to Mr. Perry Lightfoot and shake his hand. Mrs. Claus was right behind Santa. She picked up Christmas Cookie and held her, then decided to put her in her cat carrier. Santa and Mrs. Claus both shook Perry's hand, then Santa said, "Hello, Perry. So how have you been all theses years?" Perry looked down; he knew that the Clauses had heard him talking to Joshua and Lacey and that kitten. Perry looked at Santa and replied, "Well, Santa, I know you heard what I said to Joshua and Lacey, and from what the kitten looks like, I bet she belongs to Joshua and Lacey. We will be okay, I guess. It will be a little hard on us three until I find another job around here."

Mrs. Claus looked at Santa and back at Perry. Mrs. Claus asked, "Perry, what type of work do you do?" Perry looked at Mrs. Claus with a big smile on his face then said, "I am a jack of all trades and a master of none. You need it fixed, I can do it!"

Santa was listening to Perry and thought for a few seconds, then said, "Perry, I have a job for you at the North Pole. If you want it, there is only one catch: that both Joshua and Lacey come and live with you. We will build you a home next to the castle so Christmas Cookie can come and see her Mom and Dad any time she wants."

Perry could not believe what he was hearing. Santa was offering him a home and a job all at the same time! Perry put out his hand and started to shake Santa's hand to the point it was almost lifting Santa off the basement floor.

After both men stopped shaking hands, Santa said, "Okay, Perry, it's time to go. I would suggest you write a letter to the people that own the building and let them know you have moved, also that you quit. Leave the note on your bed." Perry pulled out an old, green canvas duffel bag and started to pack all his clothes; that did not take him long to do.

Santa then said, "I will be right back. I have to go to Mrs. Claus' sleigh and get one cat carrier for Joshua and Lacey to travel safely back to the North Pole." Santa put his right index finger alongside of his nose, and up the furnace vents he rose. In a flash, he was back with one large cat carrier in hand. Perry looked at Santa and Mrs. Claus and said, "Santa, can we use the stairs that lead to the roof?"

The Clauses looked at each other and Mrs. Claus said, "Sure we can, the reason we go this way, Perry, is so people do not see us." Santa reached down for the handle on the large cat carrier that held Joshua and Lacey before putting his right index finger alongside of his nose, and up the furnace vents he rose again. At that moment, Lacey let out two meows that were heard coming from the furnaces vents and then coming from the roof. In a flash, he was back for the next cat carrier that held Christmas Cookie before rising through the furnace vents a third time.

As Santa was doing this, Perry started to walk up the stairs to the roof. Santa had one more trip to make, to get Mrs. Claus. Santa appeared standing next to the furnace. He held out his left hand and said, "Well, my dear, it's time to go. I think Perry should be on the roof now." Santa looked out the window of the basement to see the sky outside was starting to get brighter. Mrs. Claus walked to her husband of many years; she raised her hand to meet with Santa's left hand. She stood next to him as Santa put his right index finger alongside of his nose—up the furnace vents they rose.

Perry was just coming through the hatch in the roof as Santa was helping Mrs. Claus into the front seat of her sleigh. Perry stopped and looked around as if to say "Goodbye, I am moving on." Perry headed to the sleigh and climbed into the back, where Joshua and Lacey were in their cat carrier. Mrs. Claus turned to look into the back of the sleigh, and she said, "Perry, you are going to need to cover that carrier. And put on you winter gear, it's going to be getting colder as we approach the North Pole." Perry opened his green duffel bag and pulled out a winter coat and gloves, as well a pair of winter boots. He put everything on.

Santa was sitting in the passenger seat of Mrs. Claus' sleigh. Mrs. Claus was about to get underway with Penny and Taz. Mrs. Claus raised the reins to say the magic words. At that moment, both Penny and Taz looked towards the sleigh, as if to say to Mrs. Claus, "Can you let Santa have the reins again for our flight home?" Mrs. Claus looked over at her husband and said, "Here, my dear, can you fly us home? I feel really tired." Santa looked at his beautiful wife and said, "Oh, of course, my dear. I think you better make an appointment with Doctor K-9 when we get back." Santa took the reins from Mrs. Claus.

Santa was happy to take the reins; he looked at Mrs. Claus said, "My dear, can you say the magic words that get your reindeer on their way?" Mrs. Claus said in a nice, clear voice, "Okay Taz, okay Penny, it's time to up, up and away! Fly, fly away!" followed by a slight jerk on the reins. Mrs. Claus' sleigh slowly pulled off the rooftop of the apartment building, and as the sleigh was starting to climb into the sky, the sun rose behind them. Mrs. Claus grabbed the microphone off the holder that was on her dash of the sleigh. She was about to call Jennifer to let her know that they were on our way home.

A green light appeared on Jennifer's tracking board on the wall. Jennifer took the microphone in her right hand and pressed on the transmit key and called to Santa Sleigh Two to do a radio check. "North Pole tracking centre to Santa Sleigh Two, do you copy?" Jennifer moved to her keyboard to update who was on the sleigh to put into the flight log. A woman's voice came on the air and said, "Hello, Jennifer. This is Santa Sleigh Two checking in. We have the following on board: Santa, Christmas Cookie, Mrs. Claus, also one man named Perry, and more cats. They are Christmas Cookie's parents; we are heading to the North Pole." Mrs. Claus released the microphone key. Jennifer replied, "Hello Mrs. C, thank you for the update. We hope all eight of you have a safe trip. This is Jennifer out." Mrs. Claus put the microphone back on its hanger on the dashboard as she was looking at Santa.

Santa was looking towards the north to see the northern lights as they were dancing in the night sky, and thought to himself, "It's time for a good old-fashioned Santa Challenge!" Santa said, "Mrs. C, I think we better have Doctor K-9 on the landing field to take our new guests to the hospital, and we need to get a hold of Donna Northern Lights. We need a home built for Perry, Lacey and Joshua to live in, and I want it built next to the castle before we land."

Mrs. Claus picked up the microphone again, to get a hold of Jennifer to let her know what Santa's wishes were. Jennifer asked, "Mrs. Claus, we know that Donna will ask how tall Perry is." Perry was listening to all that was going on. Mrs. Claus turned and looked back towards Perry and asked, "Perry, how tall are you?" Perry was surprised at this question. Perry replied, "Well, Mrs. Claus, I'm six foot two." Mrs. Claus pressed the button to transmit the information back to Jennifer.

After receiving the information, Jennifer called Donna to let her know what Santa wanted and needed to be finished before they arrived back at the North Pole from Canada.

As the telephone receiver was ringing in Jennifer's ear, waiting for Donna to pick up, Jennifer was watching the big tracking board on the wall. The green dot was slowly making its way to the North Pole. Then someone said, "Hello?" Jennifer said, "Hello, Donna? Jennifer here. I have a message from Santa for you and you don't have time to mess around. You need to call all of your elf crews and you only have a few hours to get this job done." Donna answered, "Okay, Jennifer. What is the message?" Jennifer informed, "Okay, Donna; this what Santa wants." After Jennifer passed on Santa's message, she then said, "Santa Sleigh Two is now approaching Yellowknife, NWT."

Donna had a surprised look on her face as she was writing down Santa's message. Donna's pulse went up and she thought to herself, "So we are going to have a Santa Challenge. Donna whispered under her breath, "Bring it on, Santa!" Donna thanked Jennifer for letting her know, and she had better get the house built ASAP. Both elves said good-bye to each other and hung up the telephone receivers.

Donna stood up from her desk and looked at the clock on the wall. It was 6:45 a.m. Donna headed towards the office door. She had to head to the workshop that was in the next building. She knew the crews were working on building a few new homes, but nothing this big in the history of the North Pole. Donna was not going to let the Clauses and the newest residents of the North Pole down. She called Jennifer back.

The telephone was ringing on Jennifer's desk. She reached over and said, "Hello, Jennifer here at the North Pole tracking centre, how can I help you?" Donna responded, "Hi, Jennifer. How much time do I have until Santa Sleigh Two arrives?" Jennifer looked at the board and then said, "Donna, you have two and a half hours left. You better get your jingle bells moving, girl!" Donna replied, "Oh, don't you worry, we will have that house built."

As Donna was speaking into the cellphone, she turned on the countdown timer for two hours. Donna's eyes were looking into the sky. After she hung up, Donna started to run to the workshop as fast as her little legs would take her.

Santa was looking up at the stars as they were slowly fading with the dawn sky behind the sleigh. Mrs. Claus looked down at Christmas Cookie's cage. She was busy talking and her parents were talking back, as if to say, "We do not want to be here." Both Mrs. Claus and Perry tried to calm all three cats down, but it was not working too well.

Mrs. Claus looked at Santa and asked, "My dear, why are we slowing down?" Santa had a little grin on his face as he said, "My dear, we have to give Donna and her crew of elves a chance to get Perry's new home built before we arrive." Then Mrs. Claus and Santa started to laugh. Perry had a funny look on his face, as if he was not getting the joke.

Mrs. Claus looked at her two reindeer; they looked as if they were having fun pulling her sleigh for Santa. Mrs. Claus had to ask, "Santa, how are Penny and Taz doing pulling my sleigh?" Santa looked over towards Mrs. Claus and said, "Well, my dear, Penny and Taz are great reindeer. With a few more years of flying your sleigh, they'll be ready for my sleigh one day." This put a smile on Mrs. Claus' face. Mrs. Claus looked towards the eastern sky; the sun was coming up fast behind Santa Sleigh Two. Christmas Cookie noticed a light fog coming from her mouth every time she said something. She looked through the bars at Mrs. Claus, then she looked back towards Santa. This was all new to Christmas Cookie, because the last time she was in Santa's sleigh, she was in Santa's toy sack where it was nice and warm. In the back of Santa Sleigh Two, Perry was trying to calm Lacey and Joshua down, as they were meowing all the way back to the North Pole.

Meanwhile, back at the North Pole, Donna was gathering all the elf team leaders that were in change of house building for the residents of Christmas Town. She called everyone from carpenters to plumbers to electricians to drafting elves and more! Donna was calling everyone. She was on her e-pad, talking to the nightshift elf crews, when there was a call from Jennifer. Donna had to take this call. Donna said, "Hello, Donna here, how can I help you?" Jennifer responded, "Hi, Donna. You have caught a break. Santa must have run into a headwind; you now have two hours and 15 minutes. I will let you know when they are one hour and 45 minutes away, how does that sound?" Donna said, "Thank you, Jennifer, for the Santa update. Talk to you in a few minutes."

As Jennifer hung up, she realized there was no noise in the background of elves working. Donna had her back up against the wall as the elves were coming in. She crossed her legs, with her left foot tapping on the floor. As she was tapping her left foot, you could hear a bell ringing with each tap of her foot hitting the floor. Her hands were on her hips, her head was moving from side to side, looking at an empty space in the middle of the workshop. At that moment, Donna's phone rang. It was Doreen O'Shea. Donna answered the call and said, "Yes, Doreen, how can I help you?" In a strong Irish accent, Doreen replied, "Aye, Donna, are you saying this young man is six foot two in height? Our windows are going to have to be made in Christmas Town, and our glassmakers are not sure they will have all the windows done and ready to install." Donna paused for a moment. She put her right hand behind her head, just under her elf hat, to scratch the back of her head for a moment and said, "We can always put the windows in later. We have two hours left on the clock."

Doreen said, "Okay, Donna, you're the boss, but we will have to hope that the glassmakers can get the windows done in time or this will be our first loss in the Santa Challenge." Donna replied, "I know, Doreen. We just have to hope they can make it." Donna said, "Goodbye, Doreen." Doreen hung up the phone and went back to drafting. This building would be half the size of the castle! As she picked up her drafting pencil, she started to hum a song called "Too-ra-loo-ra loo-ral", an Irish lullaby.

Donna paused as she came back into the house-building workshop. Her arms were crossed, and her e-pad was in her handbag that carried everything that Santa and Mrs. Claus might need. She started to think, "There's not enough elves here!" She grabbed her e-pad out of her handbag and called the team leader for the night shift and any spare elves she could find.

As the drafting elves were finishing up the design of Perry's new home, the lumber was being brought in with the rest of the carpenter elves. Donna and Jim were just waiting for the blueprints. Donna was pacing back and forth. At that moment, the alarm bell went off on her cell phone to let Donna know she had one hour and 55 minutes to go until the Clauses arrived home.

Donna shut the alarm off.

Doreen O' Shea came out of the drafting room, holding the blueprints in her right hand and waving them in the air. She was also singing "Danny Boy" as she looked for Donna, who was standing next to Jim, the head carpenter elf. At that moment, Donna's e-pad received a text. It was from James Jackson, the foreman to get the foundation ready for the house. Hi, Donna. The site is ready for the building, as per your instructions. Donna texted back, Thank you, James. We will be heading that way shortly.

The rest of the shift were all in now. Donna had a smile on her face for a few seconds, then that smiled faded away when a sinking feeling hit her elf tummy. In her mind, she could still hear the tic toc of the clock in her office. Donna realized, "Where is Perry going to sit, sleep, cook?" She got on the e-pad to all industries of the North Pole and got them all cranked up to make sure Perry's new home was furnished as well. Another text message came in from Dawn, the North Pole seamstress: Hi, Donna. We are up to the challenge you gave us. We will have Perry's bed made and bedding in before your house is built, and we will beat the furniture makers as well. Donna texted back, Okay. Thank you, Dawn.

A few seconds later, another text came in from Max, the head furniture maker. Hello, Donna. Don't you concern yourself with the furniture crew. We will have all the furniture in Perry's new home before the bedding gang has all the bedding out of their shop! Donna texted, Thank you, Max.

Donna stepped outside the workshop to see every light was on in Christmas Town, and all the shops had their lights on and smoke coming from all of their chimneys. Donna thought to herself, "This is the first time all of Christmas Town has come together in a Santa Challenge, and we are going to do it!"

Donna even got a text from Kelly, the flight operation manager at the reindeer barn. Kelly texted, Hi, Donna. I heard you need some lifting power. My crew and I are willing and able to help with your building. Donna texted, Thank you, Kelly. We will be heading to the site very soon. I will send a massive text out for all to come.

Gary from the snow cats and snowmobiles office texted Donna too. Hi, Donna. All our equipment is ready to go. Just say the word. Donna texted back, Okay, we need you to arrive now, and thank you.

At that moment, Jennifer sent a text to Donna. Hi, Donna. You now have one hour and 50 minutes until Santa Sleigh Two arrives. Donna read the text from Jennifer and her tummy started to warm up as if a fire was burning inside of her and thought, "We are going to get this home done!"

The sounds of a fleet of diesel snow cats and snow-clearing equipment could be heard coming from one direction. Another sound could be heard coming from another direction from Santa Kennel. It was all of Santa malamutes; their barking was getting closer to the workshop as well.

Everyone was ready to move to the site of Perry's new home. The sound of jingle bells could be heard overhead. Donna looked up to see all of Santa's reindeer coming, and they had their harnesses on, to carry items under them as they flew.

Jennifer texted, Hi, Donna. You now have one hour and 45 minutes until Santa Sleigh Two arrives at the North Pole. Donna read Jennifer's text and put her e-pad back into its case in her bag. In her mind, she could hear the tic toc of the clock in her office.

Donna jumped onto the back of one of the snow cats and slapped the dome of the snow cat to tell Charlie Chow, the driver, that it was time to go. Donna put her left hand on a handle that was on the snow cat and she turned to wave at all the crews to start. Donna then yelled, "ROLL OUT, EVERYONE!" into her megaphone, and she waved her right hand forward.

In the direction of Perry's new home, combined sounds were heard of malamutes barking and starting to pull their sleds filled with building supplies, diesel motors from the snow cats revving up, jingle bells ringing from all the reindeer that had wood rafters strapped to their harnesses. The rest of Christmas Town was bringing everything now.

Back onboard Santa Sleigh Two, Santa asked Perry, "Hey, Perry, are you getting cold back there?" Perry said, "No, Santa." Perry was too busy with Joshua and Lacey to notice the cold. He was also looking at the view of the ice below the sleigh; every once in a while, he would see some Artic animals running to get away from the sound of the jingle bells that were ringing with every movement of Taz and Penny. Mrs. Claus reached into her travel bag on the floor of the sleigh and pulled out a large thermos of hot chocolate. Santa looked over to see Mrs. Claus pouring two hot chocolates. Santa started to laugh and said, "Perry, do you know what I call that bag Mrs. Claus carries?" Perry was listening to Santa; he did not know the answer. Perry replied, "No, Santa, what do you call that very large red bag?" Santa then said, "I call it her Magic Travel Bag. If I ever run out of gifts on December 24th, I know I will find more gifts in that bag." Then both men started to laugh. Mrs. Claus did not laugh, as she was reaching for the third cup out of the bag.

Jennifer's eyes were watching the big world map on the wall. The green dot was leaving Canadian air space. Jennifer turned to her keyboard to send a message to Donna. At that moment, there was a vibration in Donna's handbag that was next to her left hip. She pulled out her e-pad and read the message from Jennifer: Donna, Santa Sleigh Two has now left Canadian air space, you have one hour and 15 minutes until they arrive.

At that second, Donna's mind was back in her office, where she could hear the tic toc of the clock and see the second arm moving closer to zero, when the Clauses would be home. Donna slapped the top of the hood of the snow cat and yelled, "We have to go faster; we need to get to the site now." Charlie Chow was driving, and he pushed the pedal to the floor of Mrs. Claus' snow cat. His head snapped back and so did Donna's, while the North Pole wind blew in their faces. Donna's elf hat was blown straight back with her long grey hair. Donna turned her head and looked to see the rest of the columns were keeping up, and there were a hundred reindeer flying overhead, doing the heavy lifting. Santa's malamutes were pulling sleds of wood and sheets of drywall, and the snow cats were bringing the logs for the walls of the cabin. She yelled, "Keep them rolling!" as she pulled her hair away from her face. Donna thought, "We are going to make it, I know we are!" All the elves and the building supplies were at the site now, ready to be put together for Perry's new home.

Jim climbed off his snowmobile so he could get this Santa Challenge done. "We will get this house built with lots of time to spare," Jim thought. It did not take Jim long to get the elf crews working and getting the walls up on the first floor.

Another text from Jennifer came in. Jennifer texted, Donna, Santa

Sleigh Two is now one hour and five minutes away. Donna replied with a text: Thank you, Jennifer. Work has started, first floor walls are up and we are just starting on second floor. Can you let me and my super team of Christmas Town elves know every ten minutes?

Donna ran back to Mrs. Claus' snow cat. She also called for teams of Santa's malamutes and half of the snow cats to head back to the workshop for another load of supplies. Donna jumped into the back of Mrs. Claus' snow cat. As the snow cat was leaving the building site, Donna looked back to see the rocks going in for the fireplace. She slapped the top of the snow cat's roof and this told Charlie to floor it. The snow cat was approaching the workshop; all the furniture was there, wrapped and ready to be shipped to the new house.

Donna and Charlie were on the way back to the building site again. Donna watched the reindeer help put up the rafters on Perry's new home from the back of the snow cat as it approached the building site, with the next wave of items for Perry's new home coming behind them. Donna started to think about the clock in her office—the sound of the tic toc and the sight of the second arm moving closer to zero, when the Clauses would be home.

Jennifer was checking on the weather when the radio came to life. It was Mrs. Claus, checking in to see how the Santa Challenge was coming. Jennifer said, "I'm not sure, Mrs. Claus. I will check for you, if you'd like?" Mrs. Claus looked at Santa to see him shaking his head in a no motion. Both Jennifer and Mrs. Claus said goodbye on the radio.

Lacey and Joshua were getting cold now, as Santa Sleigh Two headed deeper north to its final destination. Mrs. Claus was concerned for all three cats. She looked into Christmas Cookie's carrier to see there was lots of room for all the cats to keep warm. Mrs. Claus asked Perry to pass Lacey and Joshua up to the front. "We are going to put all of them in the same cage to keep warm." Santa started to speed up; he gave Taz and Penny a snap of the reins.

Jennifer was busy watching the green dot on the world map. She noticed that the sleigh was starting to gain speed on its way home. Jennifer grabbed her keyboard to send a text message to Donna. There was a vibration on the outside of Donna's leg; she reached into her handbag. Jennifer's text said, Hello, Donna. You now have 55 minutes left, and Santa Sleigh Two is picking up speed.

This put a very large smile on Donna's face, as she watched everyone working. Donna thought to herself, "Bring it on, Santa!" The sound of jingle bells were heard overhead as the reindeer brought the windows for Perry's home.

Perry had handed both of Christmas Cookie's parents to Mrs. Claus, then handed her a blanket to cover the cat carrier. As Mrs. Claus was putting on the second blanket, she lifted the first one to see all three of the cats were sound asleep. Mrs. Claus said, "Well, Perry, all three of them are sound asleep." At that moment, snow started to fall, and the wind was picking up as well. Mrs. Claus looked at Santa and asked, "How much farther?" Santa looked up at the last of the fading stars and said, "Well, my dear, we are 40 minutes away." Mrs. Claus looked back at Santa and said, "Santa, these little one are cold, and I see Perry is starting to get cold as well. No more slow motion—let's get home, so we all can have a nice supper and introduce Perry to his new home. I know that Donna will be laughing and saying, 'Bring it on, Santa!'"

Santa listened to his wife of so many years. With a turn of his head, resting his right ear just above his shoulder, he gave Mrs. C a wink and said, "Well, my dear, we are going to see what Penny and Taz can do with a fly-by of Christmas Town over the castle." Santa let out a "Ho, ho, ho! Merry Christmas!" Then the two tiny reindeer took off like never before. The snow and ice on the ground became a blur of northern lights colours that surrounded Santa Sleigh Two. That only lasted a few seconds—Santa Sleigh Two was now over the North Pole. And Christmas Town was under them next. Santa was heading towards the castle and Perry's new home.

Jennifer was about to take a sip of her hot chocolate; she was looking up at the large world map. The next thing Jennifer knew, the front of her shirt was hot and wet as she had spilled her hot chocolate on her brand-new shirt. She was watching Santa Sleigh Two take off; it was now over the North Pole and Christmas Town! Jennifer reached for her keyboard to send Donna a message, but it was too late.

Donna heard the sound of jingle bells coming from the south of Christmas Town. Santa Sleigh Two was about to do a fly-by and a right turn over the castle and Perry's new home. All the elves, malamutes and reindeer were standing near the house, looking up as Santa Sleigh Two did a fly-by. Mrs. Claus and Santa waved to everyone on the ground. Perry was shocked to see the size of his new home that was not that far away from the castle. At that moment, Mrs. Claus looked into the back to see Perry's face and the surprised look. Perry noticed Mrs. Claus looking at him; he was speechless. The only words he could come up with were, "Thank you."

Donna headed for Mrs. Claus' snow cat and was dragging Charlie Chow with her. She had to head to the reindeer barn before the Clauses landed! At that moment, Donna looked up into the sky to see all the reindeer giving Taz and Penny an escort back to the barn.

Santa turned Santa Sleigh Two towards the reindeer barn and started to descend with the other reindeer flying close by.

Donna was on the back of the snow cat. Charlie turned the key and started her up, and he pushed the pedal down; great, big rooster tails of snow came from the treads of the snow cat and buried Canyon and his team under the shower of snow. Aunty Joe was also under that mountain of snow. Canyon started to pull, and all his teammates got the sled free and wanted to head after the snow cat. But Aunty Joe had to stop them.

Santa was starting his final approach as the other reindeer started to descend as well. At the last minute, Santa changed direction, because the hospital was now under Santa Sleigh Two.

Donna and Charlie were taking the back way to the reindeer barn, when Donna saw Santa was heading to the hospital. Donna slapped the top of the roof of the snow cat. Charlie stopped, sending Donna into the cab of the snow cat; this winded her for a second, then she called out, "We need to go to the hospital. NOW!" Charlie slammed the pedal hard to the floor, then heard a bang that came from the back of the snow cat. The bang Charlie heard was Donna flying and hitting the back of the box of the snow cat, and the only word heard all over Christmas Town was, "CHARLIE!" When the snow cat arrived at the hospital, Donna looked up into the sky to see the back of Santa Sleigh Two back in the air and heading towards the reindeer barn.

Donna grabbed the handle at the top of the cab of the snow cat. She then slapped the cab one more time and Charlie and she were off again. Donna was about to fix her hair, when out of the corner of her eye, Donna saw the back of Mrs. Claus' long red coat walking into North Pole Hospital. She thought, "This is where I get off," and she ran to the back of the snow cat and jumped out of the box. She did a tuck and rolled, rolled, rolled until she stopped in a snowbank.

She stood up. Donna looked down the snow road to see the snow cat was driving away. Donna started to run into the hospital to be with Mrs. Claus and the new residents of Christmas Town. Doctor K-9 and a few nurses took the carriers to the back of the hospital, and Perry was taken to the back as well, for a check-up.

Mrs. Claus saw Donna coming through the emergency doors to the hospital; she did not look her best! Her hair was unkempt, her elf hat was hanging off of her head with some snow inside the rim, her glasses were not sitting properly on her face and her elf belt was broken, so she had to hold up her pants. As she approached Mrs. Claus, Donna tried to fix herself up with each step. Mrs. Claus asked, "What happened, Donna? Are you okay? Do you need to see Doctor K-9?" Donna replied, "Hello, Mrs. Claus. No, I'm fine. How are you doing, and how was your flight home?" Then three different screams came from the emergency room. Mrs. Claus knew who caused that! That told Mrs. Claus that Christmas Cookie and her parents were just fine. This put a little smile on Donna and Mrs. Claus' faces.

Homemade Christmas Cookie

```
E  F  O  O  U  B  U  N  W  F  E  P  A  D  H
G  N  Y  I  V  X  W  N  P  L  M  O  N  Q  S
F  H  C  H  S  A  S  W  Z  Y  L  U  T  C  R
J  G  E  V  H  E  N  J  E  N  N  I  F  E  R
W  U  F  K  B  S  G  N  Z  A  B  I  D  T  E
L  N  I  H  C  G  X  L  O  E  X  E  O  J  W
C  Q  N  O  K  N  N  N  X  D  C  B  C  Y  O
B  N  K  U  O  M  D  A  E  Y  I  Y  T  U  J
D  A  W  S  O  N  C  R  E  E  K  I  O  L  O
D  E  O  E  S  B  R  K  G  H  R  Q  R  Y  S
P  G  L  S  F  A  M  Y  N  L  S  O  O  N  H
C  O  L  L  S  R  E  E  I  Z  O  D  Y  U
V  B  E  S  M  E  W  C  L  F  C  Y  D  R  A
F  Y  Y  F  A  M  N  A  L  G  B  S  J  R  K
S  M  J  Q  E  E  U  L  A  D  D  O  A  E  S
V  I  B  H  C  N  G  G  H  D  T  E  E  P  X
Q  W  K  B  T  T  R  P  C  O  X  P  J  T  W
```

DONNA	CHALLENGE	PERRY
DOCTOR	E PAD	DAWSON CREEK
FLY	JENNIFER	HOUSE
JOSHUA	LACEY	BASEMENT
YELLOWKNIFE	O'SHEA	DOREEN

Robin White

CHAPTER 10

Letters to Santa

H ello from the North Pole. Santa here. I have been sitting here in my den, reading all the lovely letters from the children of the world. I can't find the time to sleep, as each letter warms my Christmas heart and the Christmas spirit is rejuvenated in me.

Here is a letter from Ellie and she is asking how I am doing, as well as Mrs. Claus.

Dear Santa:

I would like to thank you for the pair of skates you gave me last year and a pair of earrings for Mom and a tie and a shirt for Dad and for my sister a brand−new pair of ballet slippers. I can't wait to tell you my Christmas wishes in our community hall once again.

Thank you Santa,

Ellie

Here is another letter from Little Loretta.

Dear Santa:

I would like to say hello again. I was telling my friends all about my visit to see you and Mrs. Claus last year. I was scared of you a little bit but I talked with Mrs. Claus and she told me a secret and to watch how your tummy goes up and down when you hear those magic words and I was not to say it too loud because you would get hungry. I plan to be a big girl when I come and see you and I will say those secret words in your ear one more time.

Merry Christmas, Santa.

Love, Loretta

Here is one from little Jeff and his big brother Marcus and little sister Gwenna. Oh, those three kids I wonder what type of mischief are they up to now?

Dear Santa:

We don't want anything for Christmas this year, but can you please give our dad a new handsaw as we accidentally broke his old one doing a magic trick.

Thanks for listening.

Soon to be your new elves.

Jeff, Marcus, & Gwenna

I hope you will do something nice for others during this special season of giving.

Mrs. Claus and I enjoy reading every letter that comes to us. We hope everyone has a very Merry Christmas. Ho, ho, ho!

Love,

Santa and Mrs. Claus

Letters To Santa

```
K  R  G  M  F  F  A  L  M  Y  B  A  P  J  E
D  D  E  Y  Z  R  U  C  O  S  Q  T  S  A  H
O  R  E  I  N  V  I  G  O  R  A  T  E  D  X
C  J  H  M  S  F  S  E  L  L  E  B  T  P  B
L  Y  C  F  R  C  P  T  N  L  Q  T  N  W  C
P  Y  H  H  E  W  H  Q  A  D  R  K  T  H  M
X  L  R  U  P  A  M  I  S  O  S  I  I  A  E
X  T  I  K  P  S  F  R  L  F  R  D  G  E  Y
V  R  S  G  I  D  M  R  E  D  I  S  O  Z  O
L  H  T  K  L  N  T  U  A  R  R  G  T  F  L
S  W  M  H  S  A  S  I  T  I  C  E  E  S  E
I  S  A  P  T  H  T  A  Y  I  D  T  N  H  T
I  E  S  N  E  R  R  Q  B  A  R  B  P  I  T
Z  V  A  Y  L  Q  Y  D  W  E  Q  I  V  R  E
S  L  B  H  L  G  I  B  Y  C  Z  F  P  T  R
F  E  I  T  A  R  F  V  H  O  J  S  C  S  S
D  R  R  Q  B  O  W  M  K  C  V  Z  H  Y  V
```

REINVIGORATED	CHRISTMAS	SPIRIT
LETTERS	HAND SAW	KIDS
AFRAID	BIG	GIRL
FRIENDS	CHILDREN	LORETTA
SHIRT	BALLET SLIPPERS	ELVES

CHAPTER 11

Wake up, Karrie! Santa was Here

The sky was bright blue, and there was not a cloud in sight. Karrie and Marvin were walking home from school. Today was the last day of school for Christmas break. The teachers let them go home at noon. Karrie was talking to Marvin about her day in school and all the things she had learned.

As the two were walking, Marvin waited for Karrie to take a breath; then Marvin said, "Karrie, what did you get Momma and Papa for Christmas?" Karrie looked at her older brother, then said, "I bought Momma a scarf and some perfume that she likes; Papa, I bought him a tie and a chess set." Marvin was looking at his baby sister as she asked him, "Marvin, what did you get Momma and Papa?" Karrie had her books in her arms and her arms were crossed. Marvin said, "Well, you know, I bought them this and that." Karrie stopped dead in her tracks. She looked right at Marvin and thought, "You have not even started your shopping, have you? And today is December 22nd!" Marvin asked, "Karrie, what is the matter?" Karrie said, "Nothing!" They both started walking to the last corner and turned. They were half a block away from their house. When they were close to the house, Karrie looked to see a figure in the window. It was Momma, doing the dishes in the kitchen sink. She looked through the window to see the kids coming home for lunch, as they did every school day at this time.

Later that afternoon, Karrie went out to the backyard to lay on the fresh cut grass with her back up against a tree in the backyard of her parents' home. She was looking up at the clouds and their shapes in the sky while sucking on a Tootsie Pop. Her dog, a large Samoyed named Snowball, was already out back, lying in the shade next to the fence; he was watching her and the candy in her mouth. Snowball walked over to the tree and sat next to Karrie. Karrie had to keep telling Snowball, "Snowy, you can't have a lick of my Tootsie Pop!" After he heard what Karrie said, he lay down next to her, and she was petting the back of his head. Karrie decided to write a letter to her friend Mrs. Claus, telling her how the family was doing and how she was doing in Grade 3. Karrie started her letter by saying: *Dear Mrs. Claus, my best friend.* Snowball looked up at Karrie, just to check on her and the candy that was still in her mouth. Snowball made sure she was safe, put his head down between his front paws and went back to sleep. Raider the cat was sitting on the step to the back door, watching Karrie and Snowball; he got up and headed over to find a soft lap to go to sleep as well. Karrie started to yawn. She looked over at her flower she had planted in Momma's garden a red calla lily. Her eyes were getting heavy, so she put her pencil down and fell asleep. The Tootsie Pop fell out of her mouth and landed next to Snowball. He watched the candy on the ground, right next to his right paw.

The sounds of birds singing in the fruit trees and the smell of all the different flowers, tickled Karrie's ears and nose. When a gentle breeze touched each petal on the flowers, the scents carried through Momma and Papa's backyard and into the house sometimes. That is why Momma and Papa loved planting together, in their special garden. Karrie and Momma loved to take care of the gardens and flowerbeds every day, their most special place in the world. Karrie could hear a woman's voice calling her, "Karrie," in a soft tone in the distance. It was a woman's voice she had heard before. Karrie turned her head to the left and to the right, looking for the person that was calling her. Karrie called out, "Hello? I'm here, Momma." Then something cold and wet hit her on the end of nose. It was Raider, putting his cold, wet nose on Karrie's. Karrie called out again, "Hello? I'm here."

Karrie was about to call "hello" a third time when she heard Momma calling her to come into the house, because it was supper time. Karrie looked around to see she was in her backyard, with Raider lying on her lap. Snowball started to walk towards the back door, where Momma was standing with one hand holding the screen door open. She called again, "Karrie, come in the house. Time for supper, and you need to get washed up." Karrie called back, "Okay, Momma. I'm coming."

Karrie touched the tip of her nose; it was dry. She had been dreaming, but it seemed so real. Karrie looked up at the sky to see the sky; it was still clear. Karrie thought as she walked back to the house, "What am I missing, or was something wrong?"

Karrie slowly walked to the back door of the house, carrying Raider; Snowball walked next to Karrie. Snowball wagged his tail, and his ears were perked right up; his head held high as he looked back towards the old tree to see the empty Tootsie Pop stick laying on the ground. Karrie got to the door; she gave Momma a big hug and said, "I love you, Momma." Momma looked down at her little girl and smiled as she went down on one knee to return the hug, then said, "I love you too, my baby girl." They both entered the house and headed towards the kitchen. Momma had turned the stove down and Karrie headed for the sink and washed up, as Momma wanted her to do. Momma asked, "Karrie, can you get the table set for supper?" Karrie said, "Okay, Momma." As Karrie was setting the table, Papa came into the house from working on the old Chevy three-quarter-ton truck. He was getting it ready for an oil change and giving it a minor tune-up. As Papa passed Momma standing in front of the stove stirring the gravy, he gave her a kiss on the back of her neck. This surprised Momma and sent a shiver down her back; she spun around, giggled and looked towards the sink, where Papa had his back towards Momma, washing up as well. Momma had one rule: you come to the table clean if you want to eat.

Marvin came through the back door as Karrie finished putting the plates and silverware on the table. Marvin headed right for his spot at the dinner table. Karrie just looked at her older brother and smiled, because when Momma saw him, with his dirty face and hands, he would have to go and wash. He would have to take that dirty shirt off and go put a clean one on too. Momma told Marvin to get cleaned up and get back here for supper.

As the family was eating, Papa put his fork down next to his plate of food and looked at the family, eating and talking amongst themselves. Papa said, "Well, my family, I have news for everyone about Christmas." Karrie, Marvin and Momma stopped talking and looked at Papa. He then said, "We are heading to Grandma and Grandpa's house for Christmas Eve and Day, as well as Boxing Day. We will be coming home on December 27th. So, Momma, we are not putting up a tree inside or decorations outside the house!" This took Karrie, Marvin and Momma by surprise; there was not a word said. Karrie got up from the kitchen table, picked up her dishes and put them into the sink for Momma. Karrie did not say a word. She walked towards her bedroom. With tears rolling down her cheeks, she opened her bedroom door. Under the window was her little desk that Santa had brought for her last Christmas. Karrie did not know how Santa was going to find them away from home. With a blank page and some tears stains on the paper Karrie reached for her bright yellow pencil with the pink eraser and teeth marks on the end. Karrie's little fingers wrapped around the pencil, put the tip on the paper and started to write her letter.

Dear Santa and Mrs. Claus,

My name is Karrie. I live in Dublin, California, U.S.A. I have something very important to tell you. We are not going to be home this year for Christmas. We are going to be at my grandma and grandpa's house. They live in Oakland, California, in a big house with two levels, and you must walk up a hill to get to the house. It's a light blue house with a big porch that wraps all the way around.

I know this year will be extra special, because Grandma, Momma and I will also be making homemade chocolate chip cookies and will have them and a large glass of ice-cold milk ready for Santa.

I am worried that you will not find us on Christmas morning to get our cookies and milk. I do work very hard at keeping my older brother Marvin away from the cooling rack, and Papa goes to the store and picks up the carrots and apple slices for the reindeer.

Santa, here is my wish list:

* A Crissy doll with brunette hair and brown eyes. Or a Barbie doll and her dream house.

* A blue girl's bike with tassels on the handlebars and training wheels, please.

* The game Operation for my family.

* For Momma, a house coat and Papa, a new skill saw.

* As for my older brother, a new baseball glove, NFL football helmet and Lego building set.

Thank you,

Karrie H.

Momma called for Karrie to come and help her do the dishes. Papa and Marvin went into the living room to watch a football game. Karrie walked by the doorway to the living room, stopped at the entrance and looked in to see Papa in his brown, leather La-Z-Boy recliner, and Marvin lying on the couch. Karrie then walked into the kitchen to see Momma filling the double sink with hot water and soap. Momma looked down towards her daughter to see that Karrie had been crying, her eyes were red, and she had been rubbing them as well. Karrie said, "Momma, can we talk about Santa? Will he find us at Grandma and Grandpa's place? How will he find us? I have written a letter to the Clauses, and can we mail it?" The tears started once again from Karrie's eyes. Momma stopped washing the dishes and reached for a towel that was on the countertop. After Momma dried her hands, she grabbed a chair that was in front of the kitchen table and said, "What if we go to the mall tonight and give it to Mr. Claus, and then you can talk to him for a minute. How does that sound?" Karrie smiled at Momma as they finished up the last of the dishes

After the girls had finished the dishes and put them away, Momma looked up at the clock in the kitchen it was 5:30 p.m. They had time to get to the mall and see Santa. Momma called into the living room, "Hey, Papa. Karrie and I are heading to the Stoneridge mall for a bit. We will be back before 9 p.m." The only sound coming from the living room was the boys yelling at the referee about the call just made against their team. Papa replied, "Okay, dear, see you when you get back." Karrie went up to her bedroom to collect her letter to the Clauses. So, Momma and Karrie were off to the Stoneridge mall. There was one thing stopping the girls from leaving. Papa had his old truck parked behind Momma's car, so Karrie ran back into the house to get Papa's keys from the key hook in the kitchen. In a flash, Karrie was back outside, giving Momma the keys to the old Chevy truck, and they were off to the mall, talking about Christmas stuff, making cookies with Grandma and laughing. Momma was trying to make her baby girl feel a little better.

The mall was not far from the house. Momma parked the truck. As Momma was about to shut the motor off, the radio DJ said, "Santa and his wife Mrs. Claus will be at Stoneridge mall today only!" On hearing this, Karrie was out the door of the passenger side of the truck. She had to see the Clauses, to let her know that they would not be home this year for Christmas! The next thing Momma heard was the truck door slamming; the sound echoed inside the truck.

Karrie was out the door like one of Mrs. Claus' elves with a fresh batch of homemade cookies for Santa to taste. Momma had to call Karrie to slow down, because the mall was busy this time of year, with everyone Christmas shopping and seeing Santa and his lovely wife, but Karrie was not having any of this. She had to get in to see her friend Mrs. Claus. As Karrie ran towards the doors of the mall, she dropped her letter from her hand. Momma was right behind her; she picked it up and read the front of the envelope. It was addressed to Mrs. Claus, care of North Pole World. It did not take Momma long to find Karrie. She was in the line to see the Clauses. Momma tapped Karrie on the shoulder. Karrie looked up to see her letter in Momma's hand. Karrie looked into her pockets they were both empty! Karrie looked back at Momma and said, "Thank you, Momma."

Karrie took her letter; she would not let it go until she gave it to Mrs. Claus. The line was moving slowly; Karrie could see Santa, but where was Mrs. Claus? Karrie's heart started to sink as she thought, "Maybe I missed Mrs. Claus." The line was still moving. Momma looked towards the stage where Santa sat in his chair. Momma said, "Oh look, Karrie, does Santa look sad?" Karrie looked towards Santa's chair, but it was not the same. She wanted to see her best friend, Mrs. Claus. Momma and Karrie were last in line; they were looking towards the stage at Santa's chair. There was a tap on Momma's shoulder and a lady's voice asked, "Is this the line to see Santa?" Momma then said, "Why yes, it is." Momma turned to see a lady with snowy white hair with silver-rimmed glasses. She was wearing a bright red dress with fur around the collar and cuffs and a white apron. She also wore a pair of long white gloves, and she was carrying a little snowman purse.

A smile came across Momma's face. She tapped Karrie on the right shoulder and said, "Karrie, I have a surprise for you. I would like you to meet someone." Karrie's head was pointing down as she turned her body slowly to see a pair of shiny black boots and a red dress with white fur around the hem. Karrie's head slowly moved up to see Mrs. Claus. Karrie's eyes lit up like a set of Christmas lights on a Christmas tree in the middle of Christmas Town. Karrie was speechless for a moment, then she let out a scream at the top of her little lungs, saying, "MRS. CLAUS!" Her voiced carried through the mall all the way up to Santa's chair. Santa stopped and looked towards the line of children and their parents to see a young girl hugging his Mrs. C. She was at the end of the line on her knees, hugging Karrie right back.

Santa asked the family that was visiting him at his chair, "Do you have a minute? I would like to introduce my wife to your family, then we can all get a picture together." Off Santa went, from his chair to the front of the stage to the floor in one motion. In a few more steps, he was next to his Mrs. C. Santa said, "Hello, Mrs. C. How was your flight down here with Taz and Penny, your reindeer?" Karrie was taking in every word that Santa and Mrs. Claus were saying. Mrs. Claus replied, "We had a great flight down, Santa. I know this young lady has a great voice, I bet she can be heard around the world like you when you say 'Ho, ho, ho, Merry Christmas'."

Santa said, "Hello, Karrie. It's nice to meet you and your Momma, but, my dear, we must get back to my chair and see all these families."

Santa then held out his left arm for Mrs. Claus to hold, and they were off to their chairs on the stage. Karrie started to blush. Karrie was bubbling over with excitement, knowing that she was going to see Mrs. Claus. After all the letters Karrie had written to her over the years at Christmas, she was going to finally meet her! This was even more special, for she was going to hand her a letter directly! The line was taking forever, Karrie thought; with each step taken, her letter felt like it was hot off the press from the local newspaper that had to make the front page for the late edition.

Finally, the family that was in front of Momma and Karrie had finished visiting the Clauses—it was her turn! She was not going to miss this moment for the world, Karrie told herself. Santa waved Karrie and Momma to come up and see them. Santa held out his hand to take Karrie's letter; Karrie marched right by Santa with a full a head of steam, and stood right in front of Mrs. Claus. Karrie started to cry again. Her tears were rolling down her cheeks, but these were tears of excitement. Karrie handed the letter to Mrs. Claus.

Mrs. Claus asked, "Karrie! What is the matter, my girl?" Karrie said, "I finally got to meet you, after all the letters I have written to you and Santa." Karrie looked back at Santa and said, "Santa, we are not going to be home for Christmas this year. I know you are a busy man; that is why I'm giving this letter to my best friend in the world. I have written some other letters to my best friend, Mrs. Claus." Mrs. Claus opened the letter and read it aloud for Santa and Momma to hear. Karrie was wiping the tears from her eyes. After Mrs. Claus finished reading the letter, Mrs. Claus turned towards Santa and said, "Well, Santa, I have my own fan club now, like you do! I will have to come with you on more of these visits." Santa smiled. He laughed with a deep voice, and said, "Yes, my dear, you certainly do!" After they had their talk about what worried Karrie, there was only one thing Karrie wanted a picture of her and Mrs. Claus. Momma said, "Sure," so Santa left his chair to the girls and the picture was taken. Momma said, "Come on, Santa, we have to have one with you and us girls." Santa went back to his seat and one more picture was taken.

Mrs. Claus then said, "Don't worry, Karrie. Santa will find you no matter where you are on Christmas Eve, okay? But send me updates if your family's plans change, okay, my friend?" Mrs. Claus gave Karrie a wink and a smile. As Karrie and Momma were leaving the Clauses, Karrie said, "See, Momma, you did not have to worry. I knew Santa would find us no matter where we are on Christmas evening." Momma noticed there was still a little bit of worry in Karrie's voice, but Momma smiled and said, "Yes, my K. K. Lee Lee Mini Boots." It was off back home for them, but they had to make one stop first.

Momma decided to put up a Christmas tree anyways. She stopped at the Christmas tree lot in the parking lot of the mall. After they picked out a pine tree, the lot attendant put it in the back of the old Chevy truck, then the girls were on their way home. Momma asked Karrie to go in the garage and get the box of decorations so they could put them around inside the house. She was for sure going to put out the homemade pixie dolls that always sat on the fireplace mantel. Karrie was happy they were going to put up a Christmas tree, just in case Santa stopped by here, if he could not find them at Grandma and Grandpa's house. Tomorrow was Saturday morning the day they leave to go to be with Grandma and Grandpa.

Papa was outside early. He had just started the lawnmower to cut the grass, as he did every Saturday morning. Papa was pushing the old gas mower back and forth across the front yard. As he did that, Karrie looked out the living room window to see Marvin picking weeds out of the flower beds; Momma was helping him. She was pulling some weeds in another flower bed around a birch tree in the middle of the yard. Karrie heard Momma calling for her to come outside and help the family with the yard work. Karrie stepped away from the living room window and put on her little baseball cap with Betty Boop on it. Karrie put on her fall coat, and outside she went. Her job was to hold the trash bag open for Momma to fill it with the weeds she had cleaned out of the flower beds. After that little job was done, Momma said, "Karrie, get the cat carrier ready. Once we are done, we are off to your grandparents' place, okay?" Marvin grabbed the trash bags to put them at the end of the driveway.

Papa had finished cutting the lawn and went to get the dog cage for Snowball and tied it down in the box of the truck. Raider would ride inside the cab of the truck. Papa loaded Snowball into the cage, then wrapped a blanket around it. The family brought out their suitcases and a few boxes full of Christmas gifts for each other and their grandparents. Karrie was excited to see her grandparents, and she was the first one into the cab of the truck, along with Raider. Marvin got in next, along with Momma. Papa checked Snowball's cage one last time, then got in the truck and turned the key in the ignition but the old truck did not start. Papa tried it one more time.

Momma looked at Papa and asked, "What's the matter, Papa?" Papa looked towards his family and said, "I don't know what the matter is with this old girl!" Papa and Marvin got out, headed to the front of the truck and lifted the hood up. Momma got behind the steering wheel and waited for Papa to say, "Okay, Momma. Try it again." Papa did a few times, but the truck did not start.

Papa walked over to the driver's side door and started to talk to Momma. He suggested that she take her car and the family to Grandma and Grandpa's place, and he would follow within the hour. Momma agreed, and everything was transferred from the truck to her car—even Snowball, without his cage, which stayed inside Papa's truck. It did not take long to get Momma and the kids off to her parents' place, which was 60 miles away. Momma had to stop for gas, then the five of them would be at Grandma and Grandpa's place within an hour.

As Papa worked on the old truck, he thought to look for a battery in the garage. Papa headed towards the garage and thought, "Maybe it's time to trade in the old girl." But he thought some more about his truck, which was older than the kids and was the first truck that Momma and he bought together. Papa was trying to get the old truck to run, but it was dead on its axle and he was running out of time and options. Well, he had enough with the old girl, he would fix her when he got back after Christmas. He went into the house and called a taxi.

Grandma and Grandpa were busy getting the house ready for the kids' arrival. Grandma was cooking up a storm. Grandpa was busy making the beds with clean bedding, as Grandma wanted him to do. The phone started to ring. Grandpa stopped what he was doing and headed to the living room to answer it.

Grandpa said, "Hello? Oh hi, Paul. What's up?" Papa replied, "Hi, Dad. Just letting you know; June and the kids are driving up now. I will be leaving here in a few minutes. They should be pulling in in about 30 minutes or so, depending on traffic." Grandpa said, "Okay, Paul. Are you not coming for Christmas?" Papa answered, "Yes, Dad, I am, but the old truck did not want to start." Grandpa asked, "What's wrong with your truck?" Papa said, "Not sure, but I have to go if I'm going to make it there for Christmas Eve, okay? See you in a few hours." Grandpa said, "Okay, Paul. We will see you when you get here." They both said good-bye, then hung up the phone receivers in the telephone cradles. Papa heard a car horn outside of the house. He grabbed his coat and wallet, and out the door he went. As he was getting into the taxi, he checked his watch. It was now noon. He was hoping he had enough time get to the bank and the parts department at the dealership. Papa said to the taxi driver, "I need to get to a GM dealership in a hurry." The taxi driver put the cab into gear, and they were off down the road.

It did not take the taxi driver long to get to the dealership. Papa paid the driver, then ran inside. As he headed for the parts department, he spotted a brand new 1976 GM Sierra three-quarter-ton truck camper special with a 454 motor under the hood. It was silver in colour, and it was fully loaded. The price on the windshield in yellow paint was $8,000. Papa stopped and looked at the truck. Well, Papa could not pass up a good deal like that. He could fix up the old girl and sell it or use it for work, but $8,000! Papa rubbed the top of his head for a second, and a salesman came up to him and started to work on Papa or Papa was about to work on this young salesman!

Momma and the kids pulled into the driveway of Grandma and Grandpa's place. Grandpa was sitting in his La-Z-Boy chair, looking out the living room window and waiting for them to arrive.

Grandpa yelled out to Grandma, "They are here!" Grandma was checking the pot roast she was cooking with all the fixings; everything was homemade by Grandma's hands. She went to the fridge door, opened it and pulled something out that she had saved for Snowball; she put the treat into the pocket of her apron. She then pulled a tea towel from the handle of the fridge to wipe her hands as she headed for the front door to greet the family. Grandma opened her arms to welcome everyone with a big hug. Grandpa was going to tell Grandma that Paul would be coming later on, as he was having truck problems. His old truck would not start; he had to go and get some parts to fix it. Paul said he would be here before 6 p.m. Grandma said, "Well, come on in!" Grandma gave Momma and Marvin hugs and kisses on the cheek, then she did the same to Karrie. Snowball was sitting in the entrance, wagging his tail with his ears down. Grandma called Snowball over and started to pet him on the back of the head, but Snowball was not about to be fooled his nose picked up the scent of a bone inside Grandma's apron. Snowball started to bark.

Grandma was about to give Snowball a treat when she spotted the carrier and Grandma asked, "Karrie, what are you holding? Who is in there?" Karrie smiled and lifted the cage up to show Grandma and Grandpa her cat. Karrie said, "Grandma, this is Raider; we got him from the pound, and he is a good kitty." Grandma and Grandpa looked into the cage to see a black-and-white coloured cat with long, white whiskers and white socks on his paws. Raider was not happy to be taken from his home. Who were these people with white hair and those things hanging on the end of their noses? Momma said, "Marvin, go the car and bring our stuff in." Marvin replied, "Okay, Momma. Can Karrie come and help me?" Momma said, "Sure. Karrie, go and help your brother." Grandpa said, "That's okay, Karrie. Marvin and I will take care of it; this is men's work, right, Marvin?" Both Marvin and Grandpa started to laugh, then Marvin said, "Yes, Grandpa," and both of them went out to the car to unload it. When Marvin opened the trunk, and Grandpa looked to see a full trunk and the back seat just as full, Grandpa turned his head, looked at Marvin and said, "Oh my, this reminds me of when your Momma moved out, and she did not have this much stuff then! Don't tell me she wants to move back in?" Grandpa and Marvin started to laugh and they started to bring the stuff into the house.

Back at the dealership, Papa was talking to the salesman. Papa said, "Well, Pat, I don't know. Being Christmas Eve, things are a little tight for money and $8,000 is a lot of money. This is the end of the year, so I can see you dropping the price on this truck in two or three weeks. What can you do to lower the price to $7,000?" Pat looked at Papa and asked, "May I call you Paul?" At that moment, Papa knew he had this salesman. Papa said, "Sure, Pat, as long as you don't call me late for dinner!" Both men laughed.

Pat then said, "You know, Paul, this is a $10,000 unit and I have someone looking at it for $7,500." Papa thought, "Right, I bet your grandmother will only drive this truck to church on Sunday, one way." Papa said, "Well, Pat, if you have someone else that wants this nice truck, I will head to the parts department and pick up the parts I need to fix up my old truck, then head out to meet with my family for Christmas. I hope to join them before evening. Pat, what would your manger say to a cash deal going to the parts department and not being used on the sale of this truck, when he finds out?" Papa held back his smile as Pat headed to his manager's office to see about this deal for $7,000. Inside the dealership, the speakers played "White Christmas" by Bing Crosby. A few minutes later, Pat came with the go-ahead to sell the truck for $7,000. Papa shook Pat's hand and asked, "Pat, can the truck be ready to roll in 30 minutes? I have to go to the bank to get your money and get my insurance done and register the truck, then I will be back with my licence plates at 1 p.m." Pat looked at his watch; he knew the shop in the back would be closing in five minutes. Pat said, "Sure, I will have her ready to go, and with full tanks of gas, if I have to do it myself."

Papa looked at Pat with a funny look on his face. Gas tanks? Plural? He asked, "Pat, how many gas tanks does it have?" Pat said, "She has two large gas tanks for a three-quarter-ton camper special deluxe model." Papa was surprised, and he would not have to fill up on the way to his in-laws' place. Papa said, "'Bye, Pat, I will see you at 1 p.m." Both men said goodbye to each other, then shook hands, and Papa was on his way.

Snowball was playing in the back yard while Raider was tied to a tree because Momma did not want to lose him Raider was not happy. That dog got all the luxuries and fun, and what was the deal with him getting a steak bone? Raider only got a bowl of warm water! Raider looked towards the house when he heard the telephone ring. Karrie was next the telephone; she answered it: "Hello, Grandma and Grandpa's place, Karrie here." She waited for the other person to say something, but Papa started to laugh on the other end of the telephone. He said, "Hello, Karrie, this is Papa. Is Momma there?" Karrie said, "Oh hi, Papa. No, Momma and Grandma went to the store before it closed; they had to get stuff to make the cookies for Santa and carrots and apples slices for his reindeer. You know he is coming tonight, right, Papa?" Papa answered his baby girl, "Yes, my girl, I do. Can you give Momma a message? I will be leaving at 1:30 p.m., and I will be arriving at 3:00, okay, my baby girl?"

Papa hung up the telephone after he said goodbye to Karrie. He had to finish his errands and getting stuff for the family's new truck. He had used the payphone in the dealership. Pat was just coming out of the back, where the detailing shop was just finishing up with Papa's new truck. Pat walked over to let Papa know his truck was almost ready, and Papa said, "Thank you. Can you have the boys put these license plates on her, then we can get her paid for? Then I'm out of here! I have a long trip ahead of me." Pat said, "Okay, we will get these plates on her." Pat took the licence plates and led Papa to his manager for payment and making sure all the paperwork was right. Momma and Grandma were just walking in as Karrie hung up the telephone. Grandma asked, "Karrie, who was that on the telephone?" Karrie looked at Grandma and said, "That was Papa. He will be leaving home soon and will be here at 3:00." Karrie asked, "Momma, can I go outside to play with Raider? He looks mad because he is tied up to that tree." Momma and Grandma started to put the food they had bought for Christmas dinner away there was going to be a lot of food made for tomorrow! Grandma started to make eggnog from scratch.

Karrie was out the patio doors that lead to the back yard. Raider watched a mouse that was sitting just under the fence; that old mouse was just out of Raider's reach, and the mouse knew it. Then there was a splash. Snowball found a way into the swimming pool! He was having a great time cooling off. Karrie watched Snowball swimming in the pool. Raider was too busy figuring out a way to meet one-on-one with that mouse. Karrie walked over to the rope and untied Raider. Karrie talked to Raider as they walked towards the swimming pool. She was going to pet him, but the only thing Raider saw was an oversized water dish, and he was not going to drink out of that dog's bath!

Momma looked through the kitchen window. She made a fresh pot of coffee with Grandma's new coffee maker. Momma wanted one for Christmas; she asked Santa for one, along with a few other things. As the water filled up the glass carafe, Momma opened the kitchen window and yelled, "Karrie, stay away from the pool until I or your grandparents are out to watch you, okay, my girl?" Karrie looked towards the house and said, "Okay, Momma. I was only going to take Raider and sit on this lawn chair so we could watch Snowball, and I was going to pet Raider."

Papa was just leaving the dealership in his brand-new truck and thought he would listen to some Christmas music on the radio. He had to go back to the house and do a few things before he headed to his in laws' place. Within 15 minutes of arriving at home, he was on his way to his in laws' house. Papa was excited; this was his very first new vehicle. As he drove the 60 miles, he thought about what Momma would think about this deal. Well, in 40 minutes, he would have his answer, one way or another. The clock on the dash said 3:00 p.m. as Papa hit the highway and headed towards Oakland, California.

Meanwhile, up at the North Pole, in the Clauses' bedroom, Santa had the fireplace going with some pine burning inside the fire box; the smell of fresh pine filled the air, and the hurricane lamp gave the room some extra light. Santa reached for his black belt that was laying on the back of his chair. As Santa put on his big black belt, he looked into the full-length mirror. From the shadows of the room, a reflection stood right behind Santa. At that moment, he noticed his beloved wife looking into the mirror at her husband with a smile on her face. It was the type of smile with love for her husband; she believed in him. Santa put a slight smile on his face to show that he knew she believed in him, on this night and every night, as man and wife.

Santa turned around to see she was holding his hat, and something else was in her hands. Santa reached for his hat and put it on his head. The light from the fireplace filled the room as the festive couple stood in front of it. Santa looked down towards Mrs. Claus' hands. She put a letter into Santa's hand, it was addressed to Karrie. Mrs. Claus asked, "Santa, can you make sure she gets this?" Santa opened his coat, put it into his pocket and replied, "Of course, dear. I will make sure she gets it. I will leave it on the cookie tray so someone will find it." Santa then gave Mrs. Claus a hug and a kiss on the cheek. Santa looked towards the fireplace. He put his finger next to his nose; the fire in the fireplace went out, and up the chimney he rose. After Santa was on the roof, the fire in the fireplace came back to life and started to warm the bedroom again.

Santa headed to his sleigh on the ground, looked around at all the elves of Christmas Town, and looked towards his bedroom to see Mrs. Claus looking down at him. Santa then climbed into his sleigh; his nine reindeer were hooked to the sleigh, well-rested for tonight's journey. Santa looked up at their bedroom again, blew a kiss up to Mrs. Claus, then grabbed the reins and called out to his reindeer, "Light the way Rudolph. On Dasher, on Dancer, on Prancer, on Vixen, on Comet, on Cupid, on Donner and Blitzen!" Then Santa snapped the reins to his reindeer, and with the wind of the North Pole and the dancing northern lights all around them, they were off on another Christmas journey to see all the children of the world and the believers in Christmas.

Grandma started to dish up the supper, as it was 5:15 p.m. and there was no sign of Paul. Grandma thought, "I must get my family fed because we have to start making Santa's cookies and get the carrots ready for his reindeer." Momma called Karrie into the house for supper. As the three of them were coming into the house, Momma stopped Karrie and Snowball. Before Snowball was allowed into Grandma's house, Karrie had to dry him off. Karrie put Raider down on the kitchen floor; he walked into the kitchen and stopped next to the fridge, turned his head and watched Snowball getting a rub down with a with a very large towel. It almost covered him from nose to tail. Raider was not happy to see that dog get a bath and now a rub down. What next, a can of wet food? Raider headed into the living room to find Marvin.

Marvin was playing with his Lego that happened to be next to the Christmas tree. Every once in a while, he would look at the tags that were on the gifts, seeing how many were for him. Sometimes he would reach under the Christmas tree and drag a gift that had his name on it to see how heavy it was, and he even shook it to see if it made a noise. As Marvin was checking a gift, he didn't notice Karrie, Snowball and Raider come into the living room. All three stopped at the entrance. Karrie watched and could not believe what she was seeing! At that moment, Karrie said, "What are you doing, Marvin, with that gift?" Before Marvin could answer her, Snowball started to bark, and Raider started to meow, as if they knew Marvin was not to be doing that with his Christmas gifts.

Snowball would not stop barking, and Raider walked in circles, getting louder with his meows until Momma came into the living room.

Karrie had her hands on her hips. Marvin pushed his gift back under the Christmas tree; Karrie still could not believe that Marvin would try to open his presents before Christmas morning. Momma was coming into the living room to see why Snowball and Raider were making so much noise. Momma came up behind Karrie and stood behind her, looking at Raider and Snowball, who were still making all that noise and standing next to Marvin as if to say, "We caught him, Momma."

Momma said, "Okay, what is going on in here?" At that moment, both Raider and Snowball stopped making their own special music that would bring Momma to see what the kids were up to now. At that same moment, a car horn honked from the driveway. Grandpa came from the kitchen; he was walking towards the big picture window to see who was making all the noise outside. Suddenly, Grandpa started to scream in pain, jumping up and down, as he walked on Marvin's Lego pieces all over the rug. This set Raider and Snowball off again with their barking and meowing. Grandma came into the living room to see what all this noise was; it would scare Santa away from this house forever! Then Grandma said, "Okay, what is going on outside, and who is honking that darn horn?" As she said that, she looked at Grandpa was doing the Christmas "Lego two-step" in the living room near the Christmas tree. Momma told Marvin to pick up his Lego and put them away; it was time for supper. The radio was playing in the living room. After "Frosty the Snowman" had finished playing, the DJ announced, "We have a Santa report from N.O.R.A.D. Santa and his sleigh have been spotted leaving London, England, heading north." "The Little Drummer Boy" started to play on the radio. Karrie's head turned and looked towards the radio. She had a feeling in her tummy that Santa would not find her and her family here at her grandparents' house, but Mrs. Claus promised her that Santa would find her family here.

Grandma was the first one out of the house, then the rest of the family followed her. Everyone went outside to see a brand-new silver truck in their driveway. Papa stood in front of the truck with a nice, big smile on his face and looking for Momma's reaction. Grandpa and Marvin were the first to walk over to see the truck, then a few minutes later, the girls came over to see what Papa had done. Papa explained to Momma what had happened at the dealership, and what a great deal he had got on this truck. It was paid for, in full, in cash. Momma crossed her arms as she looked at the truck and back at Papa, as he tried to explain in a different way about how a great deal the family had made. Both Grandma and Grandpa were listening; Grandma just shook her head and Grandpa went over to Papa and said, "Paul, you made a great deal on this truck, I think." Grandma gave Grandpa a look, as if to say, "Stay out of this!" Karrie and Marvin were busy going through the new truck and looking through the front window. Inside the house, Raider and Snowball watched all the excitement around the new silver box with wheels. Grandpa called, "Marvin?" Marvin was sitting in the driver's seat when he heard Grandpa call. Marvin answered, "Yes, Grandpa?" Grandpa said, "Come and give me a hand to haul the rest of the boxes into the house." Marvin replied, "Okay, Grandpa. I will be right there."

Karrie walked back into the house, carrying a box, when she stopped to hear the radio. The DJ announced, "We have another Santa report from N.O.R.A.D. Santa and his sleigh have been spotted leaving Iceland." The horses in Karrie's tummy were running wild now. After she put the box down in the living room, she went running for Momma, tackled her and just about knocked her off her feet. Momma looked into Karrie's eyes to see that something was wrong. Momma knew what was troubling her K. K. Lee Lee Mini Boots. Momma took Karrie by the hand and they both went outside to talk. As the boys emptied the new truck and headed into the house, Papa stopped and looked back at his new girl, sitting in the driveway of his in-laws'. In the back yard, sitting on lawn chairs, Momma and Grandma were talking to Karrie and trying to make her feel better, knowing that Santa was coming here and bringing everyone a gift or two for under the Christmas tree. Marvin lay on his stomach, watching television with one eye; his other eye looked at the presents. Also, he had two sets of eyes—Snowball and Raider—watching him as well. He was still trying to get at the presents, to see what they were.

Grandma headed into the house. It was supper time, and everyone was getting hungry. Supper was ready. Momma and Karrie went into the house to help Grandma with supper. After the table was set, Grandma called the boys to come and get it—the only thing missing was a triangle bell on the outside of the cabin for Grandma to call the hired hands in from the barn. The DJ on the radio announced, "We have another Santa report from N.O.R.A.D. Santa and his sleigh have been spotted leaving Greenland and will be arriving on the east coast of Canada soon. Pond Inlet, North West Territories, is his next stop, according to N.O.R.A.D. Please stay tuned to this radio station for up-to-date information about Santa's location." A laugh like Santa's was heard coming through the speaker of the radio. Grandma asked, "Grandpa, can you go and shut that radio and the television off so everyone can come and eat supper? After supper, we girls are going to make Santa his favourite cookies and finish getting ready for tonight."

Marvin headed towards the dining room to be where the rest of the family was. He was just about to sit down for dinner; right behind him were Raider and Snowball, and they were not going to let Marvin out of their sight. Maybe he would drop some food off his plate for them, so he could get back to the living room alone. After supper, Grandma, Momma and Karrie started to make Santa's favourite cookies chocolate chip with lots of chips, according to Grandma. Karrie went running for the cupboard that held all of Grandma's baking dishes. It did not take the girls long to whip up the cookie dough, and Grandma used a large spoon to scoop out just the right amount for Momma and Karrie to start rolling into balls; then they would place them onto the cookie sheet. Grandma stopped, put her back against the countertop next to the sink and looked over at June and Karrie, as those two were busy finishing up rolling the last of the cookie dough.

Grandma had a couple tears coming down her cheeks as she watched and remembered when June and she would make cookies for Santa many years ago. At that moment, Karrie looked over to see Grandma quietly crying. Karrie put down her cookie ball and ran over to Grandma to give her a hug. Then Karrie said, "Grandma, it will be okay. Santa will be here because my friend Mrs. Claus promised me that Santa will find us no matter where we are in the world." Grandma placed her hands-on Karrie's shoulders and said, "I know, my K. K. Lee Lee Mini Boots. Santa will be here tonight, and your friend Mrs. Claus is right about him. He'll bring gifts for all the good boys and girls in the world." Grandpa, Papa and Marvin hauled in some firewood for the fireplace. Grandpa put the radio back on. The DJ announced, "We have

Robin White

another Santa report from N.O.R.A.D. Santa and his sleigh have been spotted leaving Boston, U.S.A." Marvin yelled into the kitchen so Karrie could hear where Santa was in the world. Karrie came running into the living room to hear the Santa report, but she had missed it. Her favourite song was playing on the radio, "Oh Holy Night".

Grandpa was making a small fire with Papa's help. After the fire was going, Grandpa turned on the Christmas tree lights. At that moment, the girls came from the kitchen to see the brightly coloured lights reflecting off the walls in the living room. The sound of the crackling wood burning and the smell of the smoke from the fireplace made the living room feel like Christmas. Grandma thought the only thing missing was the sound of Grandpa reading "'Twas the Night Before Christmas", and Grandpa was going to fix that in a few minutes. He walked towards the bookshelf in the living room, pulled his copy of "'Twas the Night Before Christmas" and headed back to the couch to start reading to everyone. Momma came back into the living room with fresh, homemade eggnog.

The DJ announced, "We have another Santa report from N.O.R.A.D. Santa and his sleigh have been spotted leaving Savannah, U.S.A." Karrie was about to take a sip of her eggnog as she listened to the report on the radio. She looked at Momma; Momma was already looking at her and winked as if to say, "Everything is okay." Grandpa fixed his glasses and opened the book to read the family's favourite Christmas story. When the story was done, Momma told the kids it was time to go to bed. Grandpa said, "If you're not sleeping, Santa will not stop here! He knows when you are awake, and he knows when you are sleeping!" All the girls looked at Grandpa! Grandma looked at Karrie and said, "Don't worry, Karrie, Santa will be here to have some of your cookies. Come with me we will go and get everything ready for him on the cookie plate with a large, fresh glass of ice-cold milk." As Karrie and Grandma came into the kitchen to check on the cooling cookies to put on the cookie tray for Santa, Marvin reached for his second cookie; his helpers kept watch in hope they would get some of Grandma's homemade cookies even a crumb. Both Snowball and Raider's heads turned towards the living room entrance at that moment. They walked towards the living room and passed Karrie and Grandma coming into the kitchen to see Marvin putting the second cookie into his mouth. Grandma's voice, in a very sharp tone, said, "Marvin, what are you doing with Santa's cookies?" She waited for an answer, hands on her hips, head tilted forward to look over her glasses and foot tapping on the floor.

Marvin was caught, so he thought he had better just eat the second cookie and try to talk his way out of this. He said, "Well, Grandma, I thought I would taste test them for Santa. I was going to leave him some on the cookie tray, honest I was, Grandma!" Karrie's eyes started to well up and she was about to cry, when at that moment, the DJ announced, "We have another Santa report from N.O.R.A.D. Santa and his sleigh have been spotted leaving Cuba. Please stay tuned to our radio station for up-to-date information about Santa's location." Karrie was mad, not at Marvin but at herself, for not watching the cookies better for Santa Marvin always went for the cookies on Christmas Eve! Grandpa was coming into the kitchen to see what all the excitement was, as well as Momma and Papa. Marvin looked down towards the floor, and this time, he had nothing to say to get himself out of this great cookie heist, as it would come to be known in the family. Momma said, "Before you both go to bed, you can open one Christmas gift that Papa will give," and everyone headed back to the living room. Papa headed for the Christmas tree and grabbed two gifts, one for Karrie and the other one for Marvin. Like a flash, Marvin dove into his wrapped gift. Karrie took her gift, sat next to Grandma and slowly opened it. Marvin was standing next to Karrie when he asked, "Karrie, do you need a hand opening your gift?" Karrie did not answer her older brother; she just shook her head to say no. Karrie knew if she opened her gift slowly, it would drive Marvin crazy. Both kids got a brand-new pair of pyjamas for Christmas morning, like they got every year.

Papa looked at Marvin and said, "Well, young man, it's time for bed for you." Marvin looked at the clock above the fireplace; it read 7:30. Papa's arm raised up and pointed towards the bedroom where Marvin would be sleeping that night.

Marvin said, "I'm sorry, Grandma and Karrie." He then gave Grandma a hug, as well as Momma, Papa and Grandpa. He said, "Goodnight everyone," and slowly went to bed, carrying his brand-new pyjamas in his right hand.

The DJ announced, "We have another Santa report from

N.O.R.A.D. Santa and his sleigh have been spotted leaving Brasilia in Brazil. Please stay tuned to our radio station for up-to-date information about Santa's location." Grandpa looked at the clock as well and called to Karrie. "My K. K. Lee Lee Mini Boots, Santa will be here tonight, if your Papa and myself have to wait on my roof to flag him down! But I know he will be here, so I think it's time to go to bed. Right, June?" Momma looked at Grandpa and replied, "Yes, Dad. Our K. K. Lee Lee Mini Boots should be going to bed as well." Karrie smiled and gave her Grandpa a big hug, then she walked over to Grandma and gave her a hug and a kiss on the cheek. But first, she wanted to make sure those cookies were next to the fireplace table and give one last look at the stockings that were hanging from the mantel.

Karrie noticed that Marvin's stocking had a hole in the bottom. Karrie went and got Momma and said, "Momma, Marvin's stocking has a hole in it and Santa won't be able to fill it!" Momma said, "Not to worry, Karrie, I will fix it. You better get to bed, my girl." Momma went to the living room to look at the stocking, then went and got Grandma's sewing kit to fix it. As Momma fixed the stocking, the song "Dominick the Italian Christmas Donkey" finished, and the DJ announced, "We have another Santa report from N.O.R.A.D. Santa and his sleigh have been spotted leaving Liberia in Costa Rica. Please stay tuned to our radio station for up-to-date information about Santa's location." Papa started to yawn and said goodnight; he was about to give Momma a kiss on the cheek when she asked, "Oh, Paul, did you bring in our gifts for Mom and Dad out of your new truck?" Papa looked at Momma said, "Yes, my dear, I did. They are already under the Christmas tree." Momma had finished fixing Marvin's stocking and put it back on the fireplace mantel. The fire was out in the fireplace; the lights were left on on the Christmas tree to help Santa see the living room and an ice-cold glass of milk and the cookie tray were left on an end table next to the Christmas tree. Karrie gave Grandma another hug and said, "Thank you, Grandma, and Merry Christmas." Grandma hugged Karrie back and replied, "You're very welcome, my girl. You need to go to bed now. Merry Christmas my K. K. Lee Lee Mini Boots." Grandma smiled as she gave her grand-daughter a kiss on the forehead. Momma stood in the doorway to the living room and watched what was going on in the living room.

The DJ announced, "We have another Santa report from N.O.R.A.D. Santa and his sleigh have been spotted leaving Mexico City. Please stay tuned to our radio station for up-to-date information about Santa's location." The radio started to play "Here Comes Santa Claus".

Karrie looked at the radio and her little tummy was in knots again; her Christmas smile was gone now. Karrie kissed Momma, Papa and Grandpa, then said, "Merry Christmas." She headed off to bed in a very slow walk, thinking about what Grandpa had said "Santa knows when you are sleeping, and he knows when you are awake." Momma and Papa, as well as Grandma and Grandpa, heard the door to Karrie's bedroom close.

Grandma then asked, "June, how would you like to go to evening Mass? We will leave these two to watch the kids. I know your father wants me to go to evening Mass so he can wrap my Christmas gifts."

Papa started to laugh; this put a smile on June's face She could remember all those years of having to wrap her mother's Christmas gifts for Dad. Papa then said, "Why don't you girls take the new truck and go in style?" Both Momma and Grandma's head turned at the same time, they both looked at Papa with "the look". Papa said, "What's the matter? You can drive it, you know." Momma said, "My car isn't blocked in, so I will take my car to church, but thank you anyway, Papa." The girls went off to evening Mass, and the boys listened to the radio for reports as Santa approached the United States. Papa poured two cups of coffee. Karrie lay in bed, looking at the ceiling. She could hear Marvin snoring in the room next to hers. It was going to be hard to go to sleep; she was still thinking about what everyone had said about Santa coming to Grandma and Grandpa's home tonight. Marvin stopped snoring; it was almost quiet. Karrie could still hear the radio playing Christmas music and the DJ still talking about where Santa and his reindeer were and how close they were coming towards Grandma and Grandpa's house.

The DJ announced, "We have another Santa report from N.O.R.A.D. Santa and his sleigh have been spotted leaving Dallas, Texas. Please stay tuned to our radio station for up-to-date information about Santa's location." Momma and Grandma heard the Santa report as they arrived at the church. Grandma said, "Those reindeer sure can move, right, June?" Momma smiled and said, "Yes, Mother." Then they went into the church for evening Mass.

Back at the house, in the kitchen, Papa was having a second cup of coffee and Grandpa was trying to wrap Grandma's gift, with little success. Papa watched this operation; it did look like an operation, the way his father-in-law measured each side of the box, then cut the wrapping paper to that size of the box. He taped all the sides of the box with individual pieces of wrapping paper!

The Mass had ended. As Momma and Grandma left the church, the priest wished everyone a merry Christmas. Momma and Grandma headed to Momma's old car; they would be home in a few minutes. Grandma turned on the radio to hear the Christmas music that had been playing all day. The DJ announced, "We have another Santa report from N.O.R.A.D. Santa and his sleigh have been spotted leaving Brandon, Manitoba, Canada. Please stay tuned to our radio station for up-to-date information about Santa's location." Momma started her car, put it into drive and headed for the exit to the street, then back to Grandma's house.

Back at the house, Papa was wrapping Momma's gift; he would look over at Grandpa, who was still doing a cut-and-paste with the wrapping paper and scotch tape on Grandma's gift. Karrie was lying on her back with her hands behind her head. Her eyes kept looking at the electric clock with its red display, saying 8:20 p.m. She could not sleep; she was trying but kept tossing and turning. The radio news said that Santa was now in Canada. Karrie happened to look at the wall to see a set of headlight beams light up the bedroom; that meant Momma and Grandma were home now. Momma shut the motor off. Grandma could not wait to see if Grandpa was still wrapping her gift. Momma was right behind Grandma, as Momma was also wondering what Papa had got her for Christmas. Did Paul help Dad wrap his gift for Mother? Grandma opened the front door to see both Papa and Grandpa having a cup of coffee and waiting for them to come home. As they listened to the radio, the DJ announced, "We have another Santa report from N.O.R.A.D. Santa and his sleigh have been spotted leaving Little Cornwallis Island, Canada. Please stay tuned to our radio station for up-to-date information about Santa's location."

Karrie was tossing and turning in her bed even more now, to the point that she got out of bed.

She paced the floor of her bedroom, then looked outside at the sky to see only the stars and a full moon. Karrie looked down towards the alarm clock to see it was only 9 p.m. She crawled back into bed to try and get some sleep, but sleep was slow to come this night. Karrie started to count Christmas cookies to try to help her go to sleep. Then she heard the radio again. The DJ announced, "We have another Santa report from N.O.R.A.D. Santa and his sleigh have been spotted approaching Bigger Saskatchewan, Canada. Please stay tuned to our radio station for up-to-date information about Santa's location." Then the radio started to play "Silent Night". Karrie was on her side now, listening to the music; her eyes were starting to get heavy, as if the Sandman had finally found her. Then she was woken up by a noise coming from the next room it was Marvin snoring again. Karrie thought to herself, "No, not now!" She pulled the pillow over her head, trying to kill the sound coming from Marvin's bedroom.

Momma and Papa were in the kitchen with Grandma and Grandpa, playing a game of cards, when Papa said, "Oh, it's going to be a long night for every one with Marvin's snoring." Momma was about to play a card when her head turned towards the bedrooms. Momma looked at Grandma and said, "I wonder if Karrie is sleeping yet? I better go and check on her." Momma got up from the kitchen table and headed to the bedroom; the closer she got to Karrie's door, the more noise came from Marvin's room. Momma opened the bedroom door to her old room, and the light from the hall filled the bedroom. As the door opened wider, Momma stood in the doorway. She looked right at Karrie with a pillow over her head and her hands pressed up against her ears, trying to stop the sound from getting to her brain. Momma knew her baby girl was still awake. Momma called to Karrie, "K. K. Lee Lee Mini Boots, are you still awake?" Karrie's head came out from under the pillow; her eyes were trying to adjust to the light from the hallway, and she responded, "Yes, Momma. I can't sleep with Marvin making all that noise!" Momma said, "My girl, grab your pillow and blankets, and come with me." Karrie had a funny look on her face as if to say, "Where are we going?" But she did what her Momma asked, gathered her bedding and followed her into the living room. Momma put her on the couch that faced the fireplace and Christmas tree that was lit up in the corner of the living room.

Momma gave Karrie a kiss on the forehead. She then headed for the radio and turned it down a bit, so it would help Karrie go to sleep. Momma said, "Merry Christmas my K. K. Lee Lee Mini Boots, and sweet dreams." Karrie looked at Momma, smiled at her and she said, "'Night, Momma, and merry Christmas." Momma turned to head back to the kitchen to finish playing the card game, when she saw Papa leaning up against the entrance to the living room. He was watching his two favourite girls in the world and making a Christmas memory he would never forget. Momma headed towards Papa; he opened his arms and gave his beautiful wife a hug, then they both looked up to see some mistletoe above them. He gave Momma a kiss and hugged her just a little tighter. He had his arm around Momma as they both headed for the kitchen to finish the card game.

The DJ announced, "We have another Santa report from N.O.R.A.D. Santa and his sleigh have been spotted leaving Santa Fe, New Mexico. Please stay tuned to our radio station for up-to-date information about Santa's location." Then the radio started to play "White Christmas". Karrie's eyes were starting to get heavy, as the Sandman found her once again. Grandpa headed to the living room to fix the fire in the fireplace for the night. As Karrie looked at the Christmas tree, a tear rolled down her cheek onto her pillow, and she pulled the blanket up to her shoulders. She heard her parents and grandparents say goodnight to each other and the sound of their bedroom doors closing.

The house was quiet; the only sound to be heard was the crackling coming from the fireplace. Karrie reached up with the blanket to wipe the tear that almost touched her pillow. The Christmas lights in each bulb shined bright as the stars and they danced with the fire from the fireplace; that sent a comforting warmth into every inch of the living room and around Karrie on the couch. Each red Christmas ball hanging off each bow and the garland that wrapped around Grandma and Grandpa's Christmas tree made Karrie feel extra special at that moment. She looked at Raider and Snowball, sleeping next to the Christmas presents, as if to protect them from Marvin until the next morning. Karrie had a little smile on her face as she finally went to sleep.

Karrie started to dream about her friend, Mrs. Claus, and what she had said to Karrie at the mall.

As the rest of the family slept in their beds, both Raider and Snowball looked up towards the fireplace. A man in a red suit and long, white beard stood in front of the fireplace! He looked around the room to see both of them looking at him, and then Santa looked towards the couch to see Karrie, sound asleep. Santa turned to the cookie tray and had a few of Karrie's cookies and washed them down with the milk. Santa reached into his coat and pulled out the letter from Mrs. Claus. Santa placed it on the cookie tray and then got to work putting gifts under the Christmas tree. Santa filled all the stockings hooked on the mantel. As Santa was about to leave, he reached into his toy sack and pulled out some treats for Raider and Snowball. He gave the treats to them. Santa headed back to the fireplace, and with a wink of his eye, he put his finger up along side of his nose and up the chimney he arose, to the roof and the sleigh, and off to the next house he flew.

Marvin was the first one to wake up. He headed right for the living room to see that Santa had been there with all the gifts around the Christmas tree. He went running to see what gifts he got this year from Santa, but stopped a few feet away, as Raider and Snowball stood in front of the Christmas tree, ready to sound the alarm if Marvin touched one gift. Marvin paced back and forth; with each pass, he moved closer to the Christmas tree. To Snowball, that was close enough! He started to bark, and this set off Raider a few minutes later, the whole house was wide awake. Everyone headed for the living room to see what was going on, and what all the noise was about. Karrie was still asleep on the couch. Momma went over and woke her up. Momma said, "Wake up, Karrie. Santa has been here! Look, my girl, see? He did not miss us!" Karrie yawned and sat up on the couch. She rubbed her eyes, trying to get the sand out. Grandma looked at the cookie tray to see a letter that was addressed to Karrie.

Grandma picked it up and said, "Karrie, this is for you. It was on the cookie tray." Karrie looked at Grandma as she handed her the envelope. Momma sat next to her as Karrie opened her letter and read it.

My Dearest Karrie,

I am very happy that you took the time to write to Santa and myself all these years. You do not have to worry that Santa will not find you at your grandparents' home on Christmas Eve. Santa said he will have a special gift for you on Christmas morning. For your question about the reindeer, they like carrots and apple slices. As for Santa, he like all types of cookies, but his favourite ones are chocolate chip cookies. He also like all types of fruit. I would like to wish you a very merry Christmas and a happy New Year.

Your best friend,

Mrs. K. Claus

P.S. Thank you for the great picture of us together at the mall. It is sitting on the corner of my desk in my office.

P.P.S. from Santa:

I also would like to say thank you for making me your grandma's cookie recipe.

Karrie started to smile as a tear came down her cheek. Karrie looked at Momma and said, "See, Momma? I told you Santa would find us!" Karrie then looked towards the Christmas tree to see a Raggedy Ann doll and a blue girl's bike with tassels on the handlebars and training wheels sitting on the floor. There was a tag hanging from the handlebars that read.

From Mrs. Claus.

Karrie could not wait to ride her new bike up and down the street!

Santa was landing back at the North Pole nice and safe, where Mrs. Claus waited for him. Once the sleigh with his reindeer had stopped, Santa got out of his sleigh and reached down to the ground to roll a magic snowball, to see Karrie and all of her family on Christmas morning. With Mrs. Claus also looking into the snowball, Santa gave Mrs. Claus a hug and a kiss, before they walked back to Mrs. Claus' snow cat and headed off to the castle.

Merry Christmas

Santa and Mrs. Claus

Robin White

Wake Up, Karrie! Santa Was Here

```
U  M  Q  I  E  S  L  C  D  W  R  K  N  E  A
O  A  K  L  A  N  D  X  A  S  Y  H  Z  R  M
W  R  C  J  S  O  K  K  O  G  E  L  D  N  D
O  V  C  T  C  W  R  T  A  U  J  I  B  M  N
U  I  N  A  C  B  S  D  S  E  S  K  V  P  A
K  N  P  M  L  A  U  N  L  C  V  J  D  Q  R
K  D  Q  V  X  L  X  R  J  Q  D  W  N  M  G
G  Y  E  J  H  L  A  O  K  Z  T  H  W  X  F
N  N  D  A  E  V  C  L  C  D  N  S  T  Z  L
B  S  I  S  L  K  T  Y  I  G  E  Q  H  E  N
U  T  A  R  E  E  L  E  E  L  E  E  T  O  G
V  J  X  Y  O  T  R  U  T  Y  Y  T  R  R  J
I  H  U  Z  N  N  C  S  I  V  E  A  A  N  C
R  E  D  I  A  R  S  Z  H  R  D  N  I  S  N
G  C  O  U  C  H  T  R  Q  I  D  N  A  C  L
V  S  D  U  W  N  K  J  H  P  P  B  P  U  M
B  X  D  S  Z  T  E  C  A  Z  C  F  W  Q  J
```

MARVIN	LEE LEE	CALLA LILY
LETTER	LEGO	NORAD
DISC JOCKEY	RAIDER	SNOWBALL
GRANDMA	GRANDPA	SNORING
DEALERSHIP	COUCH	OAKLAND

CHAPTER 12

Rena and Jenny's Adventures

The morning was cold; the sun was not quite up yet. It was Rena's turn to light the fire in the old wood stove. Daddy had the wood stacked in the wood box in the boot room; Rena looked out the window after she started the fire. She walked to the back door and opened the door to smell the air it was crisp and cold as Mother Nature started to paint the leaves deep reds, oranges and yellows. Our farm was close to Windsor, Quebec. After breakfast, Rena and her sister would help Daddy in the barn with the daily chore of milking the cows. The family cats were always there to get their two squirts of cow's milk. They also collected fresh eggs every morning. Daddy would ask them, "Girls, are we ready for Halloween yet?" They both answered him, "Yes, Daddy! Mommy has helped both of us." Jenny said, "I'm going as a monster," and Rena said, "I'm going as a nurse." This put a smile on Daddy's face.

Daddy then said, "Okay, girls, let's get all this stuff to Mommy. I know she wants to head into town to sell some eggs." As the three of them came out of the barn, it was starting to snow; the flakes were big and white. As the three of them walked towards the house, Daddy stopped and looked towards the old pond and the hill. This was the first snowfall of the year, and it always happened at Halloween time. The sisters always loved winter. Tonight, was Halloween. Daddy took Mommy into town as the girls put the final touches on their costumes. Rena could hear Jenny looking for a pair of large boots; the only pairs she could find were Daddy's, in the coat and boot room at the back of the house. Jenny came out of the coat and boot room with two pairs of boots one pair was his everyday work boots and the other were his church pair. Rena looked up at Jenny and told her, "Jenny, you better put Daddy's good boots back. He will not like it if they come back dirty." Jenny just smiled, took

Daddy's old boots back and came back with some toilet paper to stuff the front of Daddy's boots, so they would fit her.

Rena was busy making a nurse's hat, and then they went and got their pillowcases off their beds, for the cache of candy from the farms closest to theirs. Daddy would always go and get the car, and he would put a box in the back seat for each of them. They both looked funny, and Daddy could not see their homemade costumes; they were covered up with their winter coats and Mommy's homemade mittens and long scarves that were eight inches wide and two feet long. Well, the three of them were off! Mommy had a few jack-o-lanterns on the front step and a couple in the front window, to say there was candy there for all the trick-or-treaters. Mommy always had homemade candy apples and Rice Krispies squares ready for all the kids that showed up. Mommy watched her family leave the farm, the taillights of the old car fading into the falling snow.

As the girls went from farm to farm collecting candy, Daddy would park the car at the entrance to each driveway. Daddy would roll down the passenger window in the old car to hear them yell, "HALLOWEEN APPLES!" Rena had Daddy laughing in the car when he heard her say, "Trick or treat, you can smell my sister's feet!" After the girls had made their rounds with Daddy's help, Jenny and Rena looked in the back of the car to see that both boxes and their pillowcases were full of homemade candy. The ride home was going to be a while—Daddy was driving slowly home because the snow was getting deeper, and the car had to make a new trail for someone to follow, but Daddy got all three of them home nice and safe. He got out of the car and grabbed the boxes out of the back, and Jenny and Rena grabbed their pillowcases. Off to the house they went to get out of the snow.

Jenny was the first one into the house; she looked like a snowman with an extra lump on her back. Daddy and Rena came into the house at the same time. Jenny was showing Mommy all the goodies that were in her pillowcase as Daddy put the full boxes on the dining room table. Daddy then said, "Girls, I will light the fire for Mommy in the morning, because I have to get up early." This put a smile on Jenny's face, because it was her turn to light the stove. Daddy then headed for the boot room to get some wood for the stove that was in the living room. Mommy said, "Girls, it's time for bed and you both are going to have a busy day. Rena, I got a call tonight from the Legion and they want you to play the piano on Remembrance Day again, so you will need to practise. This year, Daddy and I will be there, so make us proud and make sure you honour all the brave men and women that have fought for our country!" Both the girls went over to Mommy and Daddy to give them hugs and kisses and said, "Goodnight." Then it was off to bed for them both, and Mommy and Daddy were right behind them.

Rena slowly opened her eyes; it was Saturday morning. She stumbled out of bed and hated to put her feet on the floor, because the floor was going to be cold on the bottoms of her feet. As Rena's feet were about to touch the floor, she thought she had better ask Santa for a couple pairs of wool socks. Then both her feet landed on the floor, and the floor was nice and warm. Rena remembered that Daddy had said, "Girls, I will light the wood stove for Mommy in the morning." The bedroom floor in Rena's room was right above the kitchen, and the smokestack was in the hallway to all four bedrooms. Jenny was already downstairs, eating her breakfast, and Daddy was already gone to work. Jenny and Rena finished their breakfast, then headed out to do their chores. Jenny hated to go after the eggs in the hen house, because the hens would poke the back of Jenny hands with their beaks. As Jenny was doing that, Rena milked the cows. Rena could always count on the two barn cats to meet her and the cows, so they could get their morning drink of fresh cow's milk. After Jenny got all the eggs from the hens' nests, she helped Rena with the milking of the cows; there were not many left to do. After all the cows were done, the milk cans were put on a red wagon, and after a few trips, all the milk cans were put into the next room for Daddy to pasteurize the milk.

He would be home at 9 a.m. to refill his thermos, grab a sandwich and put the fresh milk in for pasteurizing. Then he would be back on the roads, plowing all the snow that fell last night. Well, all the chores were done, so the girls went into the house. Mommy had a few chores left to finish up, and she told Rena, "Rena, go and practise your piano, and Jenny, you can come and help me finish these dishes." Jenny started to think it was time she learned how to play an instrument, so she could accompany Rena at these events, and get out of chores. But it was only

10 days until Remembrance Day, and then it would all be over. Then Jenny stopped Rena would have to practise for the Christmas shows at the school, then Midnight Mass. Jenny thought, "Oh, she's good." Daddy came into the house to pick up his thermos of coffee and his bag of sandwiches. He would be a few more hours, then home to finish with the milk in the barn. He gave Mommy a kiss on her right cheek, and out the back door he went. Jenny watched Daddy get into the snow plow, and off he went down the driveway. The last of the daily chores were done now, and Jenny asked Mommy, "Mommy, can I have some of my Halloween candy?" Mommy said, "Yes, you can, Jenny. Just two items—you don't need to ruin your lunch!" Jenny was off to the dining room table, where the candy was waiting. As Rena practised the piano, Jenny ate her candy apple and listened to her sister play. Jenny was getting tired of listening to the same song over and over, so she decided to go outside and check on the hill that Daddy would make into a bobsled hill, and all the kids would come and use it. Jenny reached into her coat pocket and pulled out some more candy. As Jenny looked down from the hill towards the farmhouse, she started to walk towards the skating rink that Daddy made every year, and the kids from the other farms would come and play hockey or just skate on the ice.

After she checked on the ice, Jenny decided to go into the barn and check on Chester, her horse. She decided to brush him down, and then she would do Rena's horse after Chester was done. Rena's horse's name was Ginger. Ginger was in her stall, looking over the rail at Chester as Jenny brushed him. Then Ginger looked towards the open barn door, and the wind slammed it a few times. Jenny went to close the door. She started walking towards a pail that hung on a post near the door—inside the pail was carrots. Jenny grabbed two carrots, one for Chester and one for Ginger. Jenny walked into Chester's stall, and held the carrot for Ginger over the wall. After the carrots were eaten, Jenny grabbed the brush and continued to work on Chester. After he was all done, Jenny went over to Ginger to gave her a good brushing, and this gave her time away from Rena's practising the piano.

While Jenny groomed the family horses out in the barn, Mommy was sitting in the parlour, listening to Rena while knitting a white, wool hat with beaded strings, so the wearer could tie the hat onto their head.

Mommy was keeping time with the music. Rena's fingers and her feet were starting to get tired. Rena looked toward the fireplace mantel, where a clock sat. She had been practising for hours. Mommy looked towards Rena then said, "Rena why did you stop playing?" Rena replied, "Mommy, my fingers and feet are hurting. Can I stop for a bit?" Mommy said, "Okay, Rena, you are done for the day. You can go outside and play with your sister." Rena said, "Okay, Mommy. Thank you." Rena stood up from the piano seat; her butt started to hurt as the circulation started to come back.

Mommy was finishing up knitting some heavy, woolen socks for Daddy's Christmas gift from Mommy. Rena went into the kitchen, then went to the sink that had a pump on it. She then went to the cupboard and grabbed a glass water jug; she put it under the spout of the pump, and she grabbed the handle and started to pump. A few seconds later, cold water came out of the spout and into the water jug. After it was full, she went over to the stove and grabbed a handle to lift the cast iron cover plates that were on the top of the stove. Rena lifted the plate that held water, and next to it was the plate for the fire box. After Rena filled the water box in the old stove, she put some more wood in the fire box, and she took a load of wood to the fireplace in the parlour. Mommy watched Rena fill the fireplace with wood. Mommy said, "Thank you, my girl. You need to go out and play now before Daddy gets home from work." Rena looked back towards Mommy and said, "You're welcome, Mommy. I'm heading outside now, and I think I'm going to get into a snowball fight with Jenny!" Mommy looked over her glasses, then said in a stern voice, "Rena, you are not going to throw snowballs at your baby sister, do you understand?" Rena had a look on her face of disappointment, but said, "Yes, Mommy." Her head was down, and she dragged her right foot in a half moon shape on the floor.

Rena was on her way out the back door to find her baby sister. As Rena looked around the farm, she noticed the small barn door was closed, so she headed towards the door to see if Jenny was in there. If she was not in there, she would give both the horses a good brushing. Rena opened the barn door to see Jenny just finish brushing Ginger; Rena stopped and smiled, then said, "Thank you, Jenny, for brushing Ginger down. Does Chester need to be brushed as well?" Jenny said,

"No, he was already done and they both had a carrot." Rena smiled and said, "Okay." Jenny went to the stall rail, grabbed her saddle and put it on Chester. Rena knew that there was not going to be a snowball fight as soon as Jenny got on her horse. Rena had to go with her, so she grabbed her saddle and put it on Ginger. On went the blanket and then the saddle. As the girls were about tie the straps that held the saddle in place, Chester and Ginger both took a deep breath in. Jenny climbed onto Chester, and the next thing she knew, she was under Chester, looking through his front legs. Rena started to laugh; then she got up on Ginger and said, "Giddy-up, Ginger." Rena gave Ginger a little kick with her heels of her boots. As Ginger walked out of her stall, she let out some air, and the next thing Rena knew, she was looking through Ginger's front legs, as Jenny was doing in Chester's stall. Both girls started to laugh. They got themselves standing up, and they tightened the straps to the saddles one more time. They then went for their ride into the country.

As the girls ride in the country was coming to and end, It was getting later, and they still had to get home, wipe the horses down and help Mommy with supper. Jenny said, "I'll race you!" and gave Chester the spurs. Chester took off. Then Rena yelled, "Giddy-up!" She snapped the reins, and Ginger took off after Chester. As the girls were racing down the long driveway, Jenny dropped the reins and Chester started to run faster; he was heading for the barn door. Rena realized that Jenny was in trouble, because the barn door was not tall enough to fit Chester and Jenny sitting tall in the saddle. Rena yelled, "JENNY, DUCK!" Chester was at full gallop now; he had just turned the corner of the barn. As Jenny was still trying to get control of Chester, Rena came flying around the corner; she stopped Ginger in front of the barn door. Chester was in his stall, and Jenny was leaning forward with her cheek next to Chester's neck. Both were breathing heavily. Jenny was slow to get off Chester her legs were shaking, and her face was as white as a ghost. Rena got off Ginger and went running towards her baby sister, yelling, "Are you okay, Jenny?" For a few moments, Jenny did not say anything. She had a blank look on her face, as the colour slowly came back into her face. Rena had her arm around Jenny's waist, and then took Jenny's left arm and put it around the back of Rena's neck. As Rena was doing this, Ginger walked past both girls and headed back into her stall. Rena helped her sister into the house to let Mommy know what had happened. Rena would go back to the barn and take care of the horses as Mommy took care of Jenny. After getting Jenny into the house, Rena was on her way back to the barn when Daddy's car came down the driveway. Daddy honked the horn on the car, and Rena looked towards the sound. She started to wave at Daddy. He honked the horn one more time as he passed Rena, heading towards the garage. Rena started to run towards the garage, to stop Daddy from putting the car in the garage for the night; he might have to take Jenny to see the doctor with Mommy. Rena started to call out, "Daddy, Daddy, I have something to tell you!" Daddy was at the garage doors, which were pulling to the side. He looked towards Rena and started to walk towards her.

They met near the back of the car and Rena told Daddy what had happened to Jenny. Daddy listened to every detail, then looked towards the house and said, "Thank you, Rena." Daddy then jumped in the car and headed towards the back door. In a few seconds, Mommy and Jenny were coming out of the back door of the house. Daddy pulled up, and Mommy and Jenny loaded into the back seat. Jenny was still white, and she was shaking now. Daddy took off down the driveway, off to the doctor's office. Rena headed to the barn; she had to take care of the horses. After Rena was done getting the horses bedded down for the night, she went into the house to make herself some supper, then was going to do some more practising on the piano. Rena knew that the doctor's office was 25 miles away from the farm. Mommy had made meat and potatoes for dinner that were still in the oven, Rena took them out. They were done just right, like Mommy always did. On the old wooden stove were some fresh-made buns, and in the fridge was a homemade chocolate cake.

Rena looked at the cake, then closed the fridge door. She thought after she had her supper, she would cut the cake and take it into the parlour with a glass of fresh milk. She could practise at same time. After Rena finished her supper, she washed up her dishes, cleaned the kitchen and put the rest of the supper in the fridge, with the exception of a large piece of chocolate cake on a plate and a large glass of milk with ice crystals floating in it. The farmhouse was filled with the music for the Remembrance Day event. Rena stopped playing, got up from the piano bench and opened the bench's lid. She went through her sheets of music to find a book from Fats Domino and she played "Blueberry Hill", "Ain't That a Shame", and "I'm Walking". When she was alone, these songs helped Rena play the faster songs. After she was done playing her favourite songs, she put the music books back into the piano bench. She was about to sit back down on the bench when she heard the car passing the house and stopping near the back door. A few seconds later, Daddy carried Jenny into the house and headed right to her bedroom upstairs. Jenny was sound asleep in Daddy's arms. Rena watched Daddy pass her as she stood in the doorway of the parlour. Mommy was right behind them. Mommy stopped, looked at Rena, then said, "Jenny will be fine. The doctor gave her something to settle down." Mommy then headed up the stairs to help Daddy put Jenny to bed. Rena went back to the piano and was about to start practising again when Daddy came down the stairs, looked in the parlour and asked, "Rena, can you stop playing the piano for tonight? Your sister needs her rest!" Rena said, "Okay, Daddy. I will watch some television." Daddy looked at her and said, "Thank you, my girl."

Daddy was hungry, so he went into the kitchen and turned on the radio that was sitting on the kitchen table. Rena could hear the announcer's voice coming from the kitchen, saying, "Hello, Canada, and welcome to Hockey Night in Canada, where the Montreal Canadiens and the Toronto Maple Leaf's are playing tonight." Rena came out of the parlour and headed towards the kitchen to see Daddy eating his supper and listening to the hockey game. Rena watched Daddy, then turned her head towards the bottom of the stairway as Mommy came down. Then the announcer yelled out, "He scored!" Rena's head turned back towards the radio that was sitting on the edge of the table. Mommy walked past Rena and headed towards the fridge and took out what was to be the family supper. She put the cold food on the counter, grabbed a small pot from the cupboard and made some gravy to put on the meat and potatoes. Daddy got up from the table and went for a second helping; this time, he was going to have some hot gravy on his supper. After Mommy and Daddy had finished their supper, they sat at the kitchen table and continued to listen to the hockey game. Rena was getting tired, and it was her turn to light the fire in the old wood stove in the morning. She went into the kitchen and gave Mommy and Daddy a goodnight kiss. After she had kissed them, she said, "Goodnight." Mommy and Daddy looked towards the entrance to the kitchen and they both said, "'Night, Rena. Sweet dreams." Rena smiled, then headed up to her bedroom; she left the door open so the heat would come into her bedroom.

Jenny woke up early; she got up and lit the fire for Mommy, so when Mommy got up, she could start breakfast. As she was lighting the fire, she heard two alarm clocks go off. One was Daddy's and the other one was Rena's, so she could get up and come light the fire. Jenny smiled; she knew she had forgotten to do something—like shutting off Rena's alarm clock this morning. Jenny started to laugh as the fire was now going. Jenny went over to the sink and put some water in the coffee pot, then went to the cupboard and grabbed a glass water jug. She put it under the spout of the pump, grabbed the handle and started to pump. A few seconds later, cold water came out of the spout and into the tall water jug. After it was full, she went over to the stove and grabbed a handle to lift the cast iron cover plates. Jenny lifted the plate that held water, and next was the plate for the fire box. Jenny put the covers back on the fire and water boxes, then walked over to the countertop and grabbed the coffee and a pinch salt to put into the coffee; that is how Daddy liked his coffee made in the morning. The metal coffee pot was now on the stove, perking. Jenny went back upstairs to get dressed and ready for church. As Jenny headed back to her bedroom, she stopped where the calendar was located on the wall near the window. She flipped the page from October to November, put a check mark on the 1st and 2nd and circled the 11th. Jenny thought, "There is only nine more days of hearing Rena play that piano."

Daddy went to get the car and Mommy did one final check on the girls to make sure they were dressed properly. Then Daddy honked the horn to let his girls know he was outside the back door of the house, and it was time to go to church. The family was loaded into the old car. Daddy pushed down on the clutch, then put the shift into drive, and the car slowly went down the driveway. It would take Daddy 30 minutes to drive to the church. The family arrived at the church in their Sunday best. As the family sat down in their pew, the minister came out of the back and talked to Daddy. Then Daddy came to Rena and said, "Rena, the Minister asked if you could play the organ, because the lady that plays is at home sick." Rena said, "Yes, Daddy, I can." Jenny was listening to what Daddy and Rena were talking about, and the first thing that came to Jenny's mind was, "Oh, she's good." Then the service started, and Rena started to play. The next thing Rena knew, the service was over, and the minister was shaking her hand and thanking her for the great job she did. Rena thanked the minister for letting her play for everyone that attended service.

Mommy and Daddy talked to the Minister. Rena went to look for Jenny, but Jenny was nowhere to be found in the church. Rena decided to see if Jenny was in the car; Rena came out of the church and headed towards where Daddy had parked the car, and she could see a head in the back seat. Rena opened the back door on the driver's side; Jenny was sitting on the passenger seat, reading her book. Neither girl spoke. Rena looked out the back window to see Mommy and Daddy coming towards the parked car. It would not be long before the car was warm and heading home.

That afternoon Jenny was watching an old snow owl sitting on the fence post in the field near the driveway from the kitchen window. A car drove by, and the owl took off. Jenny turned towards the calendar that hung next to the window. There was only one day left until Rena played at the Legion. Mommy and Daddy were in the parlour, watching a hockey game on television. Rena was upstairs, doing her homework. Jenny was standing in the doorway to the parlour when Lester the tabby cat came up behind her and rubbed the outside of her right leg. Jenny looked down at Lester; he stopped circling Jenny and sat down in front of her. He then looked towards the cupboard, where Buster was sitting. Jenny said, "Okay, guys, I will feed you. Come on, Lester. Come on, Buster." Jenny headed into the kitchen to feed the boys, and then she would head upstairs to her bedroom and do her homework for school on Monday morning.

Jenny headed back towards the parlour to give Mommy and Daddy a kiss goodnight, and said, "Goodnight, Mommy and Daddy. I will see you in the morning." She headed up the stairs. Jenny could also listen to the hockey game there, because her bedroom was above the parlour. Jenny got into her pyjamas, then grabbed her homework, but she wasn't really in the mood. She could hear the announcer calling the game and Mommy and Daddy yelling at the players, coaches and, of course, the refs. It would not be a true NHL game in their home if a pillow was not thrown at the television. Mommy and Daddy would shut the television off at least four or five times during a game. Jenny finally fell asleep before the game ended. It was 5 a.m. when the sound of an alarm could be heard ringing through the house. Rena lifted her head off the pillow, and she looked towards her alarm clock. As she reached to shut it off, her hand grabbed the clock—it was not ringing. Rena realized it was Jenny's alarm clock. Rena yelled, "JENNY! SHUT YOUR ALARM CLOCK OFF BEFORE YOU WAKE UP THE WHOLE HOUSE AND THE NEIGHBOURS EIGHT MILES AWAY!"

Mommy and Daddy were lying awake in bed, as Jenny's alarm had woken them up as well. Jenny shut her alarm off, then started to get up. She closed her bedroom door so she could get dressed. This was Mommy's cue to get up and head downstairs to get breakfast ready for her family. Daddy decided to get up as well.

He had a lot to do before they had to get Rena down to the Legion hall. Rena was still in bed and her pillow was over her head; her hands pressed the pillow into her ears so she would not have to listen to Jenny's alarm clock. This did not work so well, so Rena decided to get up and get her chores done, then get ready to play at the Legion. Mommy opened the curtain in the kitchen. The kitchen was starting to warm up and the coffee was perking on the stove. Jenny started to set the table for breakfast but stopped and listened to Dexter the rooster crow telling the farm it was time for everyone to get up. Jenny heard Daddy and Rena coming down the stairs. Buster and Lester were standing next to the stove to warm up, and Daddy and Rena grabbed their coats and boots to go milk the cows before breakfast.

Mommy put her three frying pans on the stove, and Jenny started making toast. Jenny went into the fridge to get the fresh milk for herself and Rena to drink, as well as the cream for Mommy's coffee. The smell of bacon, eggs, pan-fried potatoes and toast filled the air. Jenny pulled out the plates for Mommy to fill, and an extra plate for all the toast she had made. Mommy asked, "Jenny, go and call Daddy and your sister and let them know that breakfast is ready." Jenny said, "Okay, Mommy."

Jenny went to the back door and called out towards the barn, "DADDY! RENA! BREAKFAST IS READY!" Jenny waited a few moments, then she yelled it again, "DADDY! RENA! BREAKFAST IS READY!" There was no response, so Jenny put on her winter coat and boots and headed towards the barn. Jenny followed the footsteps in the snow that headed towards the barn that were made by Daddy and Rena.

It took Jenny a few minutes to make it to the barn; her legs were not as long as Daddy and Rena's were. Jenny finally made it to the barn. She opened the barn door to see Rena finishing the last cow, and Daddy was hauling the fresh milk into the next room to be pasteurized. Jenny called out to Daddy and Rena, "Daddy, Rena, Mommy said breakfast is ready, so come and get it!" Daddy replied, "Okay, Jenny, go back and tell Mommy we will be up in a few minutes. We are just about done here." Jenny then said, "Okay, Daddy. I will let Mommy know." Jenny closed the barn door and turned to start to go back towards the house. The snow was falling again. It was starting to pile up around the buildings on the farm. Jenny made her way back to the house. Rena had finished milking the last cow and was pouring the fresh milk into the milk can so Daddy could take it to the pasteurizer. Daddy told Rena, "Okay, my girl, you go into the house and have your breakfast, then we have to get you to the Legion for 9 a.m. I will be right behind you once I pour this can of milk into the pasteurizer." Rena replied, "Okay, Daddy. I will see you in the house and I will save you some toast!" Both started to laugh at Rena's comment.

Everyone was in the house and sitting around the kitchen table, eating and listening to the radio. The news and weather were on. Daddy was listening, as he might have to miss Rena play for the veterans. Daddy was just finishing his breakfast; he had half a cup of coffee to go, then the family would get changed and head out the door. Jenny and Rena were heading up the stairs to get ready. Mommy was all ready to go. Jenny was the first one downstairs, with Rena not far behind. Daddy came downstairs last, and the family was ready to go. Daddy asked the girls and Mommy, "Are we ready to go, and do we have everything?" Everyone looked at Rena; she looked down at her left arm, holding her music books. Rena said, "Yes, Daddy, I have all of my music books that I need to play."

Mommy then asked, "Rena, can you please double check and make sure you have your entire music?" Rena checked her list of songs one more time. This took her a few minutes, and then she said, "I have all the music that the Legion asked me to play today." Daddy said, "Okay, then let's go now!" Everyone went out to the old car and loaded in; Daddy started it up, and off they went to the Legion. As the car was heading down the driveway, it started to snow. Nice, big snowflakes were falling, so Daddy turned on the wipers as he drove down the road. They lived 25 miles away from the Legion hall. As we were driving down the road, Daddy turned the radio on. He was listening to CKTS radio station; he was waiting for the weather to come on, because he would have to plow the roads after the ceremony.

Daddy and Mommy were talking about the weather and what Daddy was going to do as Rena and Jenny listened. Mommy asked, "Daddy, are you going to plow the roads right after Rena is done playing? I can take the car home, but I need you to plow the road to the house. Can you start at the other end this time?" Daddy replied, "Okay, Mommy, we can do that." Daddy then looked in the rear-view mirror and said, "Rena, can you run the tractor? Because once I push the snow, it will be hard to move by the time I get home." Rena said, "I can run the tractor for you, Daddy!" Jenny looked towards Rena to see a big smile on her face. Mommy said, "Let's go inside so we can get a good seat!" The girls replied, "Yes, Mommy," and everyone went into the Legion hall. Rena went up to the front, where the piano was located on the stage. Mommy, Daddy and Jenny found seats in the second row. Rena started to play some music as people came into the Legion hall. Jenny crossed her legs and tapped her foot on the chair in front of her. Mommy leaned over and said, "Jenny, stop that, and put your foot on the floor." Jenny looked over at Mommy and put her foot down, sat up straight in her chair and crossed her arms.

After the ceremony, everyone got into the car. Daddy drove them to the service lot where his snow plow was. Mommy got into the driver's side of the car; Daddy came back to the car to keep warm as he warmed up the snow plow. Mommy had the radio on, playing the news; the weather would be on in a few seconds. Daddy looked towards the windshield of the snow plow it was clear of frost now. Daddy leaned over and gave Mommy a kiss, then said, "I will see you at home for supper, dear!" He gave her another kiss, got out of the car and headed to the snow plow. He climbed in and put it into gear, and we followed the snow plow all the way home. He turned in to our driveway, then cleaned it up to the house. Daddy blew the air horn on the plow and headed back up the driveway; he was off to clean the roads that would lead into Sherbrooke.

Rena ran into the house to put her music books in the piano bench compartment. She then ran upstairs to her room to change into her winter clothes. After she had changed, she headed to the key rack near the back door and grabbed the keys to the garage and the tractor. Rena climbed into the seat of the open-ended cab of the tractor. She put the key into the ignition, and the tractor started up nice and easy. Rena got down from the tractor and headed to the garage doors to open them. Jenny was outside to help her sister to open the garage doors and clean the piles of snow; maybe she'd throw a few snowballs at Rena as she was driving the tractor! Both girls pulled on the garage doors that opened to the side. Rena pulled on the inside as Jenny pulled from the outside. They had to open both sides instead of just one, because Mommy still had to put the car away in the garage. Once both doors were open, Jenny went to get Mommy. Rena drove the tractor out and started work on cleaning the driveway and farmyard. Rena was very proud of herself—this was the first time that Daddy had asked her to drive the tractor when he was not here!

The tractor had a blade on the rear of it, and a bucket on the front. Rena dropped the blade to clear a path for Mommy and the car. Mommy yelled and waved at Rena as she went by, saying, "Thank you, Rena!" Rena waved back to Mommy. After parking the car in the garage, both Jenny and Mommy closed the garage doors. Mommy headed to the pot-belly stove in the corner of the garage to start a fire in it. She then went back to the car and rolled down the windows so it would be warm inside the car when she had to go and get Daddy, after he was done plowing the country and township roads.

Jenny was busy getting her snowballs ready for when Rena drove by the barn. Jenny could hear the tractor coming. She bent down and grabbed two snowballs the tractor was getting closer. The bucket now passed the corner of the barn, and Jenny heard her name being called.

She looked up, and it was Mommy yelling, "Jenny, put the snowball down! You are not going to throw it while your sister is working!" Jenny dropped the snowballs. Rena was passing the corner of the barn, and the next thing Jenny knew, her face was suddenly cold and wet! Rena had stopped the tractor and thrown a snowball at Jenny and got her in the face! Mommy was not happy to see that, and she was going to have a talk with both of the girls!

The sun was slowly setting in the west as Rena finished working around the yard with the tractor. Rena knew she was going to be in trouble with Mommy. She would get extra chores and go to bed early, but it was worth it, and it was fun, just the same. Rena entered the back door of the house. Jenny was standing next to the table. Rena came into the kitchen from the boot room; she hung up her winter coat and mittens and put her boots on the rack that Daddy had built. Rena entered the kitchen and she knew what was coming. Mommy said in a very angry voice, "Girls, I am very upset with you both!" Mommy pointed at Jenny and said, "What were you thinking, going to throw a snowball at your sister when she is working with farm equipment? What if she had hit the barn or hit you with the bucket? And you, young lady!" Mommy pointed towards Rena now. Mommy was about to say something, then the phone rang, *RING, RING, RING.* Mommy walked over to the phone that hung on the wall next to the stairs. Mommy answered the phone and said, "Hello?" It was Daddy on the other end. Mommy told Daddy what the girls had done. Then Mommy said, "I think we should let Santa know what these two are really like!" Mommy paused, then said "I agree, Daddy. I will be on my way in a few minutes.

I will get the girls to open the garage for me so I can come and pick you up. Okay, Daddy. I will see you in 15 minutes." Mommy hung up the receiver and turned towards the kitchen to see both girls were gone. Mommy walked over to the kitchen window to see the girls opening the garage door for her. Mommy put her coat and boots on and headed towards the car. Once she got to the garage, she told the girls, "Girls, I want you to finish making supper. I will be back with Daddy in 30 minutes." Both girls said, "Yes, Mommy." Mommy got into the car and backed it out of the garage, then put it into drive. She was off down the driveway; the girls then closed the garage door. After this was done, they headed into the house to finish making supper. Rena knew this was going to be a long night. Daddy was sitting inside the workshop after he refilled the snow plow, waiting for Mommy to arrive. Daddy decided to make a pot of coffee to warm up. After the coffee was done perking in the electric coffee pot, Daddy poured himself a cup and was sat in the lunchroom on the bench, with his back up against the wall. He had his coffee in hand and was drinking it. He was about halfway done when the beam of headlights came through the window of the lunchroom. Daddy stood up and walked towards the window to see Mommy sitting in the car, waiting for Daddy to come out. Daddy finished his coffee and unplugged the coffee maker. He shut the lights off, then headed to the door to where Mommy was waiting for him. Mommy slid over to the passenger side of the car, and Daddy got into the driver's side. He leaned over to give Mommy a kiss she was not very happy!

Daddy was surprised at the response he got from Mommy. Daddy asked, "What's the matter?" Mommy just looked over at Daddy, as if to say, "This is your fault!" Mommy had to swallow the spit in her mouth before she answered him. Mommy replied, "Your daughters!" Then Daddy asked, "Ok, what did those two do now?" Mommy was still mad when she said, "Someone could have been killed because of you! Not to say the barn could have been damaged!" This took Daddy aback with what she has said. He put the car into gear, and they were on their way home. Mommy let Daddy have an earful of what happened at the farm; Mommy kept saying it over and over all the way home.

The girls had the table set and supper ready to be put into bowls. The girls had not said a word to each other after Mommy left to go get Daddy. Jenny could not take the silence anymore; she said, "Rena, what is Daddy going to do to us for punishment?" Rena was standing over the stove, stirring the gravy, and she just shrugged her shoulders. Rena did not say a word back to Jenny; she was mad at herself for not being a better big sister and letting Daddy and Mommy down the way she did. Jenny pulled the curtains back to look out the kitchen window and saw the car turning into the driveway, then heading towards the garage. Rena put some gravy into the gravy boat as Jenny got the potatoes from the pot on the stove into a bowl. The girls finished putting supper on the table. They were sitting in their chairs at the kitchen table when they heard Mommy still telling Daddy what had happened as they climbed the back steps, and the door opened. He took off his coat and boots in the boot room, then came into the kitchen.

The look on Daddy's face was the look of someone that was very disappointed in his children. He did not say a word, which made things worse. Mommy was right behind him, and she was even more upset with us. Jenny was about to say something when Daddy beat her to the punch. He said, "Girls, I don't want to hear a word from either one of you! After supper, you will clean the kitchen and do the dishes, then it will be off to bed for both of you." Mommy had a surprised look on her face and a question on the tip of her tongue. Mommy looked at all three of them, then crossed her arms and looked right at Daddy, as if to say, "Are you kidding me? Is that all you are going to say to your daughters?" Mommy then said, "Well, this matter is far from over, as far as I'm concerned!" Daddy looked over at Mommy and saw she was still steaming over what had happened. Everyone sat down to dinner; not a word was said by anyone.

Rena reached over to the radio that was next to her and turned it on for Daddy and Mommy, because a hockey game was on. Rena hoped this would make the mood in the kitchen a little easier. The announcer said, "Hello, Canada, and all of our servicemen and service women! On today's special Remembrance Day, our beloved Montreal Canadiens are playing the Boston Bruins." Mommy looked at Rena as if to say, "Shut that radio off!" Daddy just looked at the radio, because he had forgotten that there was a game on tonight. Daddy said, "Thank you, Rena, for reminding me that there is a hockey game tonight." Rena looked down at her plate, put her fork into the potatoes and gravy and said, "You're welcome, Daddy." Mommy was going to shut the radio off but decided not to because Daddy did not get to go to the games like he used to as a young man, before they had children.

The girls had finished their supper first and started to clean off the table. Mommy finished her supper and got up to help the girls with the dishes. Daddy tilted his head forward, then looked over his glasses at Mommy, then said, "Mommy, what are you doing? I told the girls to do this. You can rest tonight because these two daughters, as you told me, have a whole lot of work for the next 30 days. That means no television, no radio, and especially no activities after school! They are going to be very busy doing extra chores and schoolwork, on top of their regular chores and homework, and early to bed every night! Mommy, I want you to call the school tomorrow and tell the principal that you want our daughters to bring extra studies home." Mommy fell back into her chair at the kitchen table, with her mouth wide open. She was expecting a two-day punishment from Daddy. After the dishes were done, the floor was to be swept and washed, and the cats were to be fed, as well as the other animals on the farm. It was time for the girls to come into the house and get ready for bed after they had their baths.

Mommy and Daddy were still listening to the game. It was the third period; the score was tied at two apiece. Jenny came down the stairs first. She gave Mommy and Daddy a kiss each, then off to bed for her. 20 minutes later, Rena came down the stairs and she gave both Mommy and Daddy a kiss. Rena said to both Mommy and Daddy, "I'm sorry for throwing that snowball at Jenny while I was running the tractor. I'm very disappointed in myself for what I did!" Rena then turned and started up the stairs. As she was climbing the stairs, she had a tear in her eye, and she thought she heard Mommy and Daddy talking as she climbed the stairs. Rena and Jenny cried themselves to sleep that night.

Dexter the rooster started to crow as the sun rose in the east. Rena was already downstairs. She had the fire in the stove going; she even started a fire in the parlour because the house was cold that morning. Snow was falling outside; Rena looked out of the parlour window at the spruce trees covered in snow. The driveway was full of snow, which meant Daddy would have to go and plow the roads again. Jenny was coming down the stairs, wiping the sand out of her eyes and yawning as well. Rena then said, "Jenny, you need to wake Daddy and let him know that it is snowing, and it snowed last night." Jenny replied, "Why don't you tell him?" Rena then said, "I'm going to go start a fire in the garage and take the tractor out to clean the driveway so he can get to work. Can you make him a lunch and coffee as I'm doing that?" Rena then pointed to the fridge door and said, "There is a note on the fridge door with your name on it it's a list of extra chores for you." Rena got her winter clothes on, and as went out the back door, she grabbed the keys for the tractor. She wanted to get a path cleared for Daddy.

Jenny went back upstairs to give Daddy the message, and she hurried back to the kitchen to start to making Daddy's breakfast and lunch.

Rena took the shovel and cleared the front of the garage doors so she could open them, and she headed for the potbelly stove in the corner. She lit a fire in it and put some coal in to keep the fire going after the fire was lit. She started the tractor and put it to work cleaning the snow away so Daddy could get to work; she wanted to show Daddy that she was a responsible daughter, as Mommy would say. The tractor was really working this morning, because a lot of snow had fallen overnight. Rena was just finishing up clearing the yard on the farm when she saw Daddy coming out of the house with his lunch box and a thermos under his arm. Rena thought Jenny did a good job. Daddy thanked Rena for clearing all the snow in the yard and driveway. Daddy was getting into the family car; he put the key into the ignition. He was still holding the key and he was thinking how nice it was that his girls were helping a lot more around the farm. This gave Mommy a chance to get some rest as well. Daddy turned the key, and the car started. Daddy then got out and opened the garage door so he could back out the car. Then he would have to close it, to keep the heat inside for Rena when she was done with the tractor.

Jenny got dressed to go outside. It was time to go and collect the eggs from the hen house. Dexter the rooster did not like the girls coming in and stealing eggs from his hens. Jenny opened the door to the chicken coop. The first thing that Jenny did was look for Dexter; he always waited for her to come in, and then he would do something to her. Jenny reached into the chicken coop with her right hand and slowly moved her hand up and down on the wall, trying to find the light switch. It took her a few seconds, but she found it, and Dexter found her arm with his large talons. The fight was on! Jenny flung her arm up and down and side to side. Dexter flapped his wings as if he was on an amusement ride, but Jenny was trying to get Dexter off of her arm. The harder she tried to get him off, the harder he dug his talons in. Jenny was about to slam Dexter into the wall when he let go and landed on a perch that was in the chicken coop.

Jenny headed towards all the hens sitting on their nests, and they were all upset as well. This meant the back of her hand was going to get pecked. Jenny put on a pair of Daddy's heavy work gloves. Jenny was hoping that it would not hurt as bad when the hens pecked her. Rena was backing the tractor into the garage. She had to go and milk the cows before school, because the bus would be at the entrance to the driveway at 8 a.m. sharp. Rena looked at her wristwatch—it was 6 a.m. She thought, "This is going to be close." She went into the barn and all the cows were in there, so she did not have to go and round them up from the field. Rena thought, "Daddy must have brought them in last night." She went to work getting the cows ready for milking, and after each one was done, she put the fresh milk into the milk can.

As she was finishing the first cow, she heard a loud noise coming from the chicken coop. Rena knew it was the morning fight between Jenny and Dexter. They went at it when Jenny would go into the chicken coop, and they would fight again as she was leaving. Jenny finally got out of the chicken coop with a load of eggs in her basket. After she brought them into the house for Mommy, she would help Rena with milking what was left of the cows, then put the milk into the pasteurizer and start the machine. The girls would have to get ready for school. They would leave the cows in the barn; Daddy let them out into the corral at 10 a.m. Jenny went running into the house; she had to get changed and washed up for school, and she had to go to her bedroom to place an X on her calendar. After she did that, she said, "29 more days of extra chores!" Both girls were just coming out of the house when they saw the school bus at the top of the hill, coming towards their driveway. They both started to run down the driveway to meet the bus.

After school, the girls got off the school bus and headed up the driveway towards the house. They knew they had to get changed and work around the farm until supper time, then after supper, they had to do their homework. Then it would be bedtime for them. Rena was up early again the next morning, and she went downstairs to get the family's day started. Jenny followed her down the stairs to get her morning orders from Rena and the new list of chores from Daddy that was on the fridge door. Rena looked out the kitchen window to see if it had snowed; on the days it did not snow, she would get dressed and head out to the garage to light a fire in the garage, like she would do for the next month, then head to the barn to start milking the cows. Jenny would start to make breakfast. Some days, Rena would grab the basket and go into the chicken coop and surprise Dexter, because for some reason, Dexter was afraid of Rena. The hens would still peck the back of Rena's hand, but it did not take as long to gather the eggs and get them into the house. Jenny would have breakfast ready and Daddy's lunch and coffee ready for him. Rena came back into the house with the fresh eggs, then headed to the barn to start milking the cows.

Rena was watching Daddy drink his black coffee; she always wanted to try a cup of coffee, but Mommy said, "NO. COFFEE IS FOR HARDWORKING ADULTS!" Rena looked at Daddy, then asked, "Daddy, am I a hardworking adult?" Daddy put a forkful of fried potatoes into his mouth. He looked at Rena with a funny look on his face. Then asked, "Rena, why do you ask?" Jenny was sitting at the table as well, putting jam on her toast and wondering what Rena was going to ask as well.

Rena then said, "I would like a cup of coffee, Daddy." At that moment, Mommy's voice was heard coming around the corner into the kitchen saying, "NO DAUGHTER OF MINE IS GOING TO START DRINKING COFFEE. IT WILL STUNT HER GROWTH AND MAKE HER TEETH GO BROWN!" Daddy looked over his left shoulder to the entrance to the kitchen to see Mommy standing there with her arms crossed. Daddy looked back at Rena and said, "I guess that answers your question." Daddy looked towards Jenny and started to smile; he gave her a little wink. The only ones not smiling were Mommy and Rena. After breakfast, the girls headed out to the barn to get the cows. When that was done, they got ready for school and waited for the bus at the entrance to the driveway. Rena had her own calendar in her room with December 11th circled in red, and today was December 10th. This was the last day of doing extra chores around the farm. As Rena put her socks on, she started to think, then it hit her, "Oh, Daddy, you are really good. Jenny and I showed Mommy and you that we can work together and do a lot more work around the farm to help out. We are used to it now. Yes, Daddy, you are really good!" Daddy started to work on the bobsled run and hockey rink. Kids would come over every weekend to play hockey, and all the local boys wore their favourite Montreal Canadiens jerseys. The same number would be on the backs of the boys as they played and fought each other, saying they are that player and the other boy would say, "No, I'm that player." Daddy and a few of the other men from the nearby farms decided to fix the old bobsled run last spring. The hill was just off the corner field, and that is where Daddy and the men would make two rinks—one was for hockey and the other one was for family skating. All the kids, near and far, were getting excited to try the bobsled track with all the new S curves and the high walls that were put into it. Well, good ol' Jack Frost did not let them down!

Rena and Jenny grabbed their bobsled and headed for the bobsled track. As they were talking and laughing, they came across some boys, Ernie and Hank. They also had a bobsled in hand and were heading for the track as well. Rena looked at the rough shape of their bobsled, and she said, "Where did you get that broken-down wreck of a two by fours?" Both Jenny and Rena started to laugh. Hank looked at the girls' brand-new bobsled, and he said, "I never knew they had a pink powder puff with yellow bows on the front of it for a bobsled now?" Both boys started to laugh. Jenny and Rena looked at each other; these two boys were about to eat some yellow snow! Rena stopped in her tracks and looked at both of them, then said, "I bet we can beat you both and that termite-filled piece of wood! Here are the rules: we start with two riders, and you have to end with two riders at the finish line!" Both boys agreed. They all shook hands and headed up to the top of the run. Rena sat in the front of the bobsled, and Jenny got on behind her. The boys put their bobsled next to the girls' bobsled.

Jenny wrapped her arms around Rena, nice and tight. Rena turned her head towards her left shoulder and said, "Jenny, hang on tight. We are going to beat these two termite farmers." Jenny had a smile on her face, and she replied, "Okay, Sister. Let's do it!" Rena started the count-down "Five, four, three, two…" They yelled, "GO!" Both bobsleds slowly moved down to the first turn; the girls had a bit of a lead, but the boys were catching up. By the fifth turn, the bobsleds were dead even, and then there was bumping back and forth. Jenny kicked Hank in the ribs after he bumped their bobsled a second time. Jenny yelled, "Rena, lean forward!" This is where their bobsled took the lead in the sixth turn! There was a bump in the track that Rena hit. Jenny screamed, "R…E… N…A!" and she was bounced off of the bobsled. She hit the side of the wall and slid down into the path of the boys' bobsled. There was a bang as the second bobsled ran over Jenny, sending the boys over the wall. Jenny was limping down the track to the finish line, where Rena was waiting for her and that termite-filled bobsled to show up. Jenny was laughing as she came around the corner of the track. In her right hand was a piece of wood that come off the boy's bobsled. Jenny raised it up over her head like the Gold Olympic medal for Canada that they won in bobsled. Rena went over to her sister and put her arm around her, and they went home laughing and talking about how they beat those two boys and will do it again another time.

Mommy started to call all the neighbours to see what they were bringing for the annual Christmas gathering, when all the farm families would get together. There would be lots of food, hot chocolate and activities for everyone, from skating to races down the new bobsled track, and hockey game—the old timers versus the young guys—and a dance in the barn that was built many years ago for community events such as this. Rena was sitting in the loft, watching family and friends dancing to the Christmas music by the live band, kids drinking their hot chocolate and the adults having some hot apple cider and eggnog. At the end of the night, everyone started to clean up the community barn. When it was finished, no one wanted to go home; everyone was having a such great time. As the people were leaving, they wished everyone a Merry Christmas and a Happy New Year, and there were hugs all around. Daddy, Mommy, Rena and Jenny were the last ones to leave, because Daddy had the keys to the community barn. It was not far to walk back to the house. The snow was gently falling; there was no wind. Mommy and Daddy walked hand-in-hand, and the girls carried gifts from Santa, which every child at the party received. When they arrived home, and it was December 24th, and the grandfather clock chimed 11 p.m. Both Mommy and Daddy said, "You girls better hurry and get to bed, because Santa will be here soon." Rena and Jenny said, "We must go and get our gifts for the tree!"

They ran up the stairs and banged into each other a few times; they came out of their bedrooms at the same time, almost hitting each other again. Rena had her wrapped gifts hidden in a red blanket, and she carried it down the stairs like Santa with his toy sack. After the girls put their gifts under the Christmas tree, they said, "Goodnight, Mommy and Daddy, and Merry Christmas." The girls gave Mommy and Daddy a hug and a kiss each. Mommy and Daddy said, "Merry Christmas, our girls." The girls went up to bed; Mommy and Daddy were right behind them, and the last light in the hallway upstairs was put out. Jenny was having a hard time going to sleep. She was looking towards the hallway, listening for Santa's sleigh and his reindeer landing on the roof of the house. Everyone else in the house was sound asleep. As the grandfather clock chimed midnight, there was a soft bang on the roof over Jenny's bedroom. Jenny sat up in bed and looked at the ceiling, then jumped out of bed and ran to Rena's room to wake her up. Jenny started to shake Rena's shoulder and whispered, "Rena, get up! Santa is here! Come on, Rena, wake up!"

Rena opened her eyes, threw her bedding off to the side and jumped out of bed. They both went to the vent in the hallway floor that helped to bring heat upstairs. They both lay on the floor, looking down through the vent to see the Christmas tree below them; then the light came on in the parlour. There were two voices talking—one man's and one woman's voice were heard. The girls looked at each other. The lady was checking the stockings that hung on the mantel to find one had a hole in the bottom; the other one that was next to it did as well. "This will not do," Mrs. Claus thought, so she reached into her long coat and pulled out a needle and thread and she fixed the girls' stockings, as Santa placed gifts under the tree. Jenny moved to get a better look and she bumped the vent; this jarred a piece of dust that floated down in front of Santa.

Santa looked up to see the girls looking down at him. Santa said, "Well, Mrs. Claus, we have two wide-awake girls upstairs, you know what that means." Santa put his finger next to his nose, and the lights all went out then they were gone! Jenny and Rena ran back to their rooms to look out the windows to a clear sky and a full moon. Rena called to Jenny, "I see them, Jenny!" Jenny ran back to Rena's room just in time to hear Mrs. Claus and Santa saying, "Merry Christmas, Rena and Jenny! Light the way, Rudolph! On Dasher, on Dancer, on Prancer, on Vixen, on Comet, on Cupid, on Donner and Blitzen."

Robin White

Rena and Jenny's Adventures

```
V  S  B  J  D  U  U  O  M  X  F  O  F  C  W
N  M  X  F  E  V  N  Q  C  E  N  G  R  E  Y
M  H  Q  R  T  N  L  A  Q  C  X  H  E  V  U
S  U  L  H  J  L  N  R  B  R  E  S  N  N  Q
U  X  P  O  K  A  C  Y  T  U  O  B  A  O  N
M  D  P  B  D  E  L  S  B  O  B  T  E  A  P
K  P  N  I  T  I  C  F  V  T  W  B  G  U  H
X  D  A  S  A  D  A  O  M  W  K  G  Z  K  Q
T  N  U  A  A  N  C  P  V  W  O  I  N  X  G
Y  D  D  A  D  H  G  M  F  B  K  N  Y  K  B
K  R  V  L  E  D  O  H  O  O  J  G  O  M  D
P  Y  X  S  J  M  N  T  N  Q  E  E  P  B  I
Y  O  T  L  M  G  I  L  A  E  U  R  E  U  J
Z  E  I  Y  V  H  N  L  I  W  Y  M  Y  P  E
R  J  J  B  J  Q  T  M  P  T  K  J  C  D  M
N  E  E  W  O  L  L  A  H  C  F  W  G  W  N
W  W  O  O  D  S  T  O  V  E  K  A  M  J  H
```

QUEBEC	HALLOWEEN	JENNY
PIANO	MOMMY	DADDY
CHESTER	GINGER	CANADIAN
NHL	WOODSTOVE	DUST
BOBSLED	TOBOGGAN	RENA

North Pole Smarties Cookies

Ingredients

- 1 cup margarine
- 1 cup firmly packed brown sugar
- ½ cup white sugar
- 2 tsp. vanilla
- 2 eggs
- 2¼ cups flour
- 1 tsp. baking soda
- 1 tsp. salt
- 1¼ cups Smarties

Recipe Notes

Mix all ingredients, then add ¾ of the Smarties into batter, roll
in balls.

Put on cookie sheet (ungreased).

Put one Smartie on top of each cookie. Bake at 375°F for 10 minutes.

Mrs. Claus' Maple Syrup Muffins

Ingredients

- 1 egg
- ¼ cup milk
- 2 ½ tsp. baking powder
- ¾ cup flour
- 1 cup pure maple syrup
- ½ tsp. vanilla
- ¼ cup butter

Recipe Notes

Beat eggs, lightly add milk. Combine flour with baking powder. Alternate the additions of the dry ingredients with mixture of maple syrup, vanilla and melted butter. Thoroughly grease and flour 12 muffin cups; add batter. Bake at 350°F for 12-15 minutes.

Cabbage Raisin Salad

Eva Robinson

Servings	6
Prep Time	10 min
Passive Time	1 hour

Ingredients

- 1 small head of cabbage, finely shredded (four cups)
- 2½ cup seedless raisins
- 2 Tbsp. sugar_
- 2 Tsp. salt
- 4 Tbsp. mayonnaise
- 1 Tbsp. vinegar

Recipe Notes

Combine cabbage, raisins, sugar and salt in a large bowl; let stand for one hour to blend flavours. Drain off any liquid. Mix mayonnaise and vinegar in a cup; spoon into cabbage mixture; toss to mix well.

Corn Chowder

Ingredients

- 1 Tbsp. shortening
- ½ cup chopped yellow onions
- ½ can corn nibbles (add more to taste)
- 1 cup russet potatoes, cooked and diced
- 2 cups milk
- Butter, salt and pepper (to taste)

Recipe Notes

Fry onions in shortening. Peel and dice potatoes; cook in just enough water to cover in a double boiler. Add cooked onions, milk and corn. Add butter, salt and pepper to taste.

Boiled Fruit Cake

Eva Robinson

Servings	12
Prep Time	30 min
Cook Time	1 hour
Passive Time	30 min

Ingredients

- 2 cups raisins
- ½ tsp. clover or any kind of spice
- 1 cup brown sugar
- ½ tsp. nutmeg
- ½ cup shortening
- ½ tsp. salt
- ½ tsp. cinnamon
- 1 cup boiling water
- 2 cups flour
- 1 tsp. baking soda
- 1 tsp. vanilla
- Add peeled fruit, chopped nuts, maraschino cherries (optional)

Recipe Notes

Bring all ingredients to a boil and simmer for six minutes, or until the raisins have doubled in size. Remove your saucepan from the heat.

Place the mixture into a cake pan and bake at 300°F for one hour. After baking, let cool to enjoy.

North Pole
Ho Ho Ho Ho

Dear Santa

Thank You

Robin White

Puzzle Answers

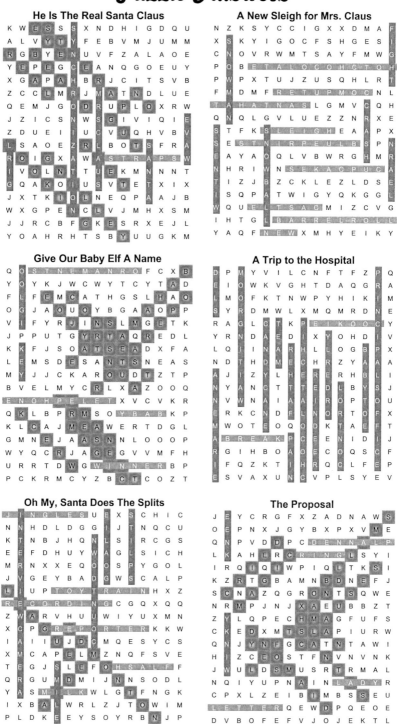

He Is The Real Santa Claus

A New Sleigh for Mrs. Claus

Give Our Baby Elf A Name

A Trip to the Hospital

Oh My, Santa Does The Splits

The Proposal

Puzzle Answers Continued

Canyon Takes A Ride

A Haircut For Santa

Homemade Christmas Cookie

Letters To Santa

Wake Up, Karrie! Santa Was Here

Rena and Jenny's Adventures

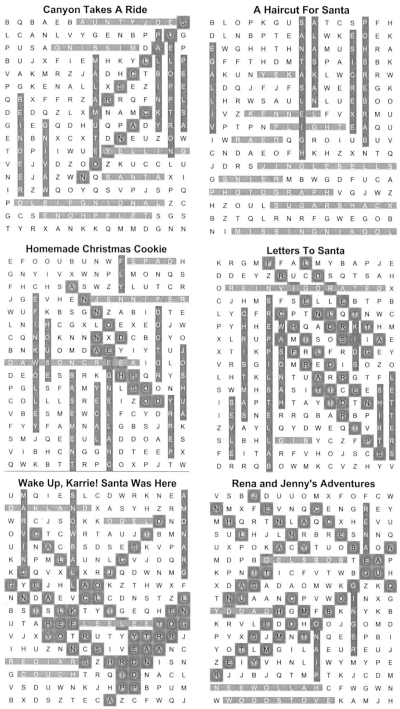

Created with TheTeachersCorner.net Word Search Maker

Robin White